GUARDED HEART

GAME TIME SERIES

BY

S.M. DONALDSON

TABLE OF CONTENTS

INTRODUCTION
NOTE FROM THE AUTHOR
DEDICATION
PROLOGUE
CHAPTER 1
CHAPTER 2
CHAPTER 3
CHAPTER 4
CHAPTER 5
CHAPTER 6
CHAPTER 7
CHAPTER 8
CHAPTER 9
CHAPTER 10
CHAPTER 11
CHAPTER 12
CHAPTER 13
CHAPTER 14
CHAPTER 15
CHAPTER 16
CHAPTER 17
CHAPTER 18
CHAPTER 19
CHAPTER 20

CHAPTER 21

CHAPTER 22

CHAPTER 23

CHAPTER 24

CHAPTER 25

CHAPTER 26

CHAPTER 27

CHAPTER 28

EPILOGUE

A SERIOUS NOTE FROM THE AUTHOR

Acknowledgements

About the Author

Other Titles by S.M. Donaldson

Excerpt From Casey Peeler

~S.M. DONALDSON~

GUARDED HEART

Guarded Heart is a work of fiction. All names, characters, places and events portrayed in this book are either from the author's imagination or are used fictitiously, with exception to brand names, artists named, and their song lyrics, and direct quotes from movies whose titles have been named. Any similarity to real persons, living or dead, or events is purely coincidental and not intended by the author.

Cover by: IndieVention Designs
Cover Image: DepositPhotos
Editing by Chelly Peeler
Paperback
ISBN-13: 978-1540345943
ISBN-10: 1540345947

INTRODUCTION

Welcome to the time where memories are made and hearts get broken.

Raven Quinn has always been a force on the basketball court, but in life, not so much. Having a dating life isn't easy when she's taller and stronger than every guy she knows, or he's already put her in the friend zone. Which hasn't really been a problem until now. Now she's feels left out and left behind. What if she's in the friend zone for the rest of her life? Shane Gibson makes her think differently and takes her out of that dreaded friend zone, but in the wrong direction.

Grant Hudson has been Raven's best friend since they were in diapers. She's the best friend a guy could have, he's always felt that way. So why does this guy she's dating bother him so much? Why is he suddenly very aware of her body and the way his reacts to her? Why, for the love of everything, can't he get her off his mind?

When things go south with Shane and Raven is broken, will Grant step up and take the shot, getting past the guard Raven has around her heart?

WARNING: This book is a Mature YA book. It is intended for people 15+, it is not suitable for those younger.

NOTE FROM THE AUTHOR

This series is very special to me. For a long time, I wanted to try my hand at Young Adult, now my hometown has inspired me to do it.

The small town I grew up in had two schools, an elementary school for Pre-K – 5th and a high school for 6th-12th. All of the surrounding towns are pretty much the same way. Growing up in a place like this is special. Every Friday night during the fall you can hear the noise and see the lights from the football stadium and once you get close enough, you can smell the boiled peanuts and grilled hamburgers from the concession stand. During the winter and early spring, the high school gym is packed out a few nights a week with the smell of popcorn wafting out the door. Spring time brings baseball and softball to life. With parents somewhere between the school fields and the recreational fields, many nights of supper are eaten from the concession stands.

Our school wasn't your typical high school with cliques. We didn't have enough people, so we were like one big clique. I graduated with just under one hundred people. That doesn't mean that we didn't have the couple of small groups of snarky people who thought they were better than everyone, but our school just wasn't segregated that way. Most of the kids in our school were on multi teams. They may cheer, but they could also be marching with band at half-time. At the end of football season a player may be leaving that practice to go straight to basketball practice. I had a great principal who thought the students shouldn't have to choose. The adults had to learn to work with the students and each other on scheduling.

So this book I hope brings a little bit of the small town world to life for you. The town where your parents know what you did before you got home from thinking you got away with doing it. You couldn't go anywhere without someone knowing your parents, the words "do I need to call your (insert…parents, Mama, Daddy, Grandma)" are scarier than the idea of getting a paddling or any other punishment and most of the time, also, the cops are just going to give you a ride home.

So here's that glimpse. I hope you enjoy it.

XOXO

S.M. Donaldson

DEDICATION

To my younger self. I'm grateful you learned not to give a crap what others thought.

PROLOGUE

Grant-

"Ouch, you fucker!" I hear as a fist slams into my shoulder.

I slam the ball into the hoop. "What was that for?"

"You elbowed me in my damn boob, asshole," Raven yells as she grabs the ball.

"You have boobs, you mean? I've never noticed them," I joke, but the basketball coming at my head says it's not a funny joke.

"Screw you, asshole," she says. Storming to her backyard, she sits in the swing hanging from the large oak.

I jog behind her. "Look, Rave, I'm sorry. I didn't mean to elbow you in the boob," I say uncomfortably. "I know you have boobs, I was just making a joke."

She glares up at me. "A shitty joke, okay? Yes, I have boobs. They may not be huge like the ones you're used to messing around with, but they're there. And your elbow fucking hurt."

"Sorry. Look, you're the best friend a guy could have. Sometimes it's just easier for me to pretend that you don't have female parts." It really is easier.

Raven and I grew up together. Hell, our parents put us in the bath together until we were six or seven. Had sleepovers until we were in middle school. That was around the time my mom had to explain to me why we woke up one morning and Raven's side of my bed had blood on it. Raven was embarrassed and I was sick to my stomach.

"Do you need me to grab some ice for you?" I ask.

She barks out a laugh. "Ice, really? For my boob? Damn, you aren't real smooth, are you? Women don't like ice on their boobs."

I sit down on the lawn chair close by. "I beg to differ. Some women get off on it."

"You're truly full of yourself, aren't you?" She fiddles with the hem of her shorts. "So I take it you and Tabitha...?"

I laugh. "We...?"

"Ugh, you know. Had sex."

"Um, yeah," I boast.

She looks at me and I can tell she's nervous to ask her next question. "What was it like?"

Fuck, now I'm uncomfortable. I tell Raven everything, she's my best friend, just like any guy I'm friends with. "It was great with her. I guess."

"With her? You mean there have been more?" she asks with an almost disgusted look on her face.

I roll my shoulders. "Well, yeah, we broke up. I've been on dates since then."

"Guys, dinner's ready!" her mom calls from the patio.

As we walk to the house, I feel a thickness between us that's never been there. I stop just outside the door and grab her arm. "Why did you want to know what it was like?"

She looks everywhere but my face as she pulls her arm away and turns to go inside. I barely hear her say, "In case I never find out."

CHAPTER 1

Raven-

I've always been great on the court. My self-confidence out there is earth shattering, but off the court not so much. I'm taller than most girls and very muscular from working out. Most guys don't find that very attractive and most girls tend to make jokes about me being a dyke. I have no problem with someone who is gay, but that's not me. The girls on my team are the only ones who don't say stuff like that and the boys on the team think of me as a buddy. It's funny, guys always bitch about being stuck in the "friend zone" and how bad it sucks. Well, they've never been a girl stuck there.

Just two more weeks of this school year and then summer break. Then I'll be starting on the Varsity team next year. Sophomore year has to be better than freshman, right?

Color me shocked when I find Shane Gibson leaning against my locker. "Hey." I motion to my locker. "I kinda need to get in there." Shane's popular, but for all the wrong reasons in my opinion. He's either banging some cheerleader or telling off a teacher. People always say he's just like his deadbeat dad, but I try not to listen to that. I only know what I see. He does smart off to teachers and if the locker room is a reliable place for info, he's great in bed. Not that I'd know what's bad in bed.

"Oh, sorry." He gives me a smirk and moves, motioning for me to go to my locker like a game show model showing off prizes. "By all means." I fight it, but end up giving him a small laugh.

I exchange some of my textbooks and he stands there leaned against the locker next to mine. "So Raven, what are you up to this weekend?" Why is he making conversation with me?

I shrug. "Not really sure." I am a freshman so it's not like I'm allowed to have a ton of plans without my parents' approval. "Some of the girls on my team have talked about going to the Springs to swim so I may do that."

"You should come out with me on Saturday night."

I have to stifle a laugh. "Seriously? You want me to go out with you?"

"What, you don't think I'm good enough?" He looks a little offended.

I quickly backtrack, not meaning to offend him or hurt his feelings. "No, sorry, I just didn't think you were really that interested in me."

He brushes a piece of stray hair from my face. The charm is back. "Why wouldn't I be? You're gorgeous, you're fit and you've got a great personality." He leans back against the lockers. "You just seem cool and like you aren't caught up in what other people think." He shrugs, "People seem to always think they know so much about me, when they know nothing."

I hate how people put others in a category and never let them out of it. I'm sure some of these girls think he's great to screw around with, but not to take home to meet their parents. "Yeah, that sounds like fun. Let me talk to my parents, though."

He gives me a smirk. "You have to ask?"

"Um." I stumble. "Yeah, don't you?"

He gives me a laugh. "If she cared that would be one thing, but she doesn't so no, I don't ask a damn thing."

I nod, feeling bad that his mother doesn't care enough to know where he goes. "I'll let you know tomorrow."

He gives me a head lift. "Good. I'll talk to you then."

One of the guys from the basketball team walks up. "Hey, what was Shane harassing you for?"

"Oh, um, actually he was asking me out for this weekend."

"I hope like hell you turned him down."

"Why?"

Cher, a girl that used to date Grant, walks up on the tail end of the conversation. "Because he's a douche and kind of an asshole."

I shrug. "I don't know what I'm going to do yet."

Cher looks at me. "Just think about it before you agree. Okay?"

I nod. At the end of the day, there is a really sweet note in my locker reminding me of how much he wants to take me out. I've never gotten a note like that. Maybe he's right and all of these people judge him too harshly, he just needs someone to try and understand him.

Saturday night rolls around and my parents have said yes to my date. A knock at the door has me nervous. I've never been on a date before. I didn't go to homecoming this year, no one asked me.

Making my way to the living room, I hear my parents talking to Shane. My dad looks at me. "Be home by eleven."

I nod. "Yes, sir."

Once we make it to Shane's truck, he opens the door for me. "By the way, you look really pretty tonight."

I smile. "Thanks."

That's the first time anyone other than my parents have ever called me pretty.

Our dates continue. Shane always tells me how beautiful I am. Well, now it's more like how sexy I am. It has caused some tension with my parents because I've been a little late for curfew a few times and Shane isn't some golden boy.

My dad was all into sports and clubs but Shane is more of a loner, Dad doesn't get that. It makes me mad because he hasn't really tried to understand Shane. I finally start dating someone who will accept me for me and Dad pushes them away.

We've been together for five weeks, and he's good to me. He treats me like I'm important. My parents don't understand him. They think we're too serious, but they don't realize how much he needs me. He has no one but me. So if he snaps at me every now and then, I can take it. He's under a lot of pressure and most adults mistake his confidence for disrespect.

Our relationship has progressed pretty fast, which is okay with me. In my opinion, I have so much to catch up on compared to other girls my age. Most of my friends are like Grant and have had sex with several people by now. I've been getting heavily acquainted with third base and he really wants to take it home.

"Babe, come on. Don't get me wrong, I appreciate the blow jobs and I'd put my fingers inside of you all day long, but I want to have sex with you." He caresses the side of my face. "I care about you, babe. I just wanna show you how much." Kissing down my neck, he says, "You're so beautiful, no one else sees you like I do."

I know he's right. "Shane, I'm just not sure if I'm ready. I mean this is a big step for me." I'm not too worried about birth control. I had to be put on it a few years ago to control my periods, it's just I don't know if emotionally I'm ready. It took all the courage I had to let him go down on me once.

He sits back, sighing with irritation. "Are you always going to be a damn little girl, Raven? Jeez. You'd think you could pop your overprotective momma's tit out of your mouth long enough to realize how good this could be. I want you. It's not like you have a line of guys out the door saying that."

Fuck, I feel like an idiot. I am acting like a child. Girls my age do this all the time. It shouldn't be a big deal. Why am I getting so damn emotional about it?

My phone vibrates with an incoming text.

Grant: We're coming over this weekend get ready to lose.

"Who is Grant?" he asks with an accusing tone.

"His parents are friends with mine. We've been friends since we were in diapers." I don't dare text him back right now.

"Are you fucking him?" he barks.

"No. It's not like that," I say with a small voice. Truth is Grant wouldn't give me the time of day like that. I'm his "best friend." "We both play basketball so we normally have a pickup game while our parents are visiting," I hastily try to explain.

He relaxes a little. "Oh yeah, I'm sure he just sees you as a tomboy like everyone else." He reaches over, grabbing my boob. "Nobody else would enjoy your tiny tits like I do."

Wow, punch to the gut. I guess he's right, though. He's the only guy who has ever shown me interest. Maybe this is it for me and my barely B cups. My brain always runs these same words over and over again in my head. I just need to move on and get it over with. Stop living in my damn head. Adjusting myself in the seat, I climb over him to straddle him. "Oh, you wanna play now," he says, removing my shirt. Soon he's got me laid across the bench seat of his truck. He roughly starts to pull my shorts down.

"Wait," I mumble out.

"Not this again." He grumbles something about being a fucking tease.

I try to recover quickly. "No, it's just the seatbelt is digging into my back." I adjust a little. I would like for him to stop, but it'll be hell if I do ask.

He grins and finishes taking my clothes off. I stare at the top of the truck, trying to mentally get myself ready for this. I hear him saying things to me, about how I'm gonna love it and he's going to show me a good time, but I can't focus on that. I hear him reach in the glove box for a condom, so at least I know that's done.

He leans down and kisses me. That's what I try to focus on when I feel the sting of my virginity going away. He says more things to me, but I'm not paying attention. Pretty soon, he's done. I'm not sure what he thought would rock my world. I felt better after he ate me out, as awkward as that was for me, but maybe this is just something that gets better.

After we're both redressed, he looks over to me. "You ready to go home now?" Wow, that was blunt, but then I look at the clock, realizing that I'm late for my curfew once again.

"Yeah. I'm gonna be late again."

Great. My parents will be really pissed now.

Walking into my house, my dad is sitting on the couch…waiting with some kind of book in his hand. "Hey, sweetie, come over here and take a look at this book with me real quick."

Why isn't he yelling? I'm almost two hours late. I sit down beside him and see it's some kind of children's workbook. He looks at me. "Okay, I thought since you seem to be unable to tell time anymore, we could review what the big hand and the little hand on a clock mean. Also, how to read digital numbers since you must have a problem with that, too. Considering that you're almost two hours fucking late walking in my damn front door."

"I'm—"

"Sorry. I know." He huffs.

"We were just hanging out with friends and lost track of time," I try to explain with a lie.

"Well, that I really wouldn't mind, considering when your mom ran into Kelly, she said that you haven't been hanging out with them this summer at all."

I shrug. "I've been hanging out with my boyfriend and his friends. That happens, you know."

The truth is my friends don't like him and he doesn't like them. He says they talk down to me and treat me like I'm less than them. They have invited me to the lake, but he doesn't like it when I go places where there will be other guys without him. I have to admit, it's nice to have someone be jealous over me of all people. And it's like he said, my body wasn't built for a bikini. He enjoys my body but others would probably just laugh about the lack of curves.

"Well, I think you guys need some space. This is too much, too fast. And tonight was the final time for being late. You're grounded."

I jump up from the couch. "What?! For how long?"

"I would say as long as it takes for you to pull your head out of your ass, but for now, two weeks."

"Where's Mom? I can't believe she agreed to this!" I yell.

He steps toward me. "Do not raise your voice at me, young lady. Your mom went to bed; she's talked to you the last few times you've come in late. She asked me to see if I could do a more effective job tonight."

"Fine." I throw up my hands and storm to my bathroom. Turning on my shower, I think about how I really wanted tonight to go. I thought my first time would be romantic. Instead, it felt rushed and uncomfortable. My parents are ganging up against me and now I have to tell the one person who appreciates me that I can't see him for a couple of weeks. Great.

CHAPTER 2

Grant-

Watching Raven warm up for our one-on-one game, I know something is wrong. "Rave, what's up? You seem, I don't know, off somewhere else."

She looks at me full of attitude. "I'm fine. It's everyone else that has a damn problem."

"Okaaay," I draw out. "Does this have something to do with you being grounded?"

"Arrrh!" She slams the basketball into my chest. "In some ways, yes."

I pass it back to her. "Check. Well, from what I heard...not that *you* told me...you were late for curfew for the fourth time since you've started seeing this guy you have yet to introduce me to." I shrug. "So I'm sure your parents are pissed."

She shoots the ball, missing the basket. "Why do you have to be on their side? You're my friend. They're just mad that someone finally shows an interest in me. Me, not me playing basketball. ME."

I steal the ball from her, which I shouldn't be able to do, but her head's not in the game. Before she says anything else, her phone rings. She darts to it. "Hey." She has this smile on her face that I've never witnessed. Maybe this guy is something she needs.

"I'm sorry," she says to the guy on the phone. I can see now she's getting upset. "I can't help it. I'm grounded." She sighs, rubbing her temples. "They said that the other night was the last straw. I mean it's only for a couple of weeks. I told you, we have company tonight anyway." I can hear his voice raised through the phone, which puts me on alert. "Shane, it's not like that, I'm not doing that with anyone else. I'm grounded so they wouldn't let me invite you over." I can see the tears in her eyes. "Fine. Yeah. I love you, too. Bye."

After she ends the call, I march over to her. "What was that all about?"

She pulls herself together. "He's just upset he can't see me. He doesn't have parents like mine, so he pretty much is his own boss. He just wants time with me. He misses me." She turns, dribbling the ball.

"He raised his voice at you, Rave!"

"It wasn't really at me, he was just irritated with not being able to see me. Plus, my parents haven't made him feel the most welcome, you know," she tries to explain. "He needs me. He loves me. He has no one BUT ME."

"Are you sleeping with him?" I stand, watching her dribble the ball.

"That's not your business, Grant." She stops dribbling and slams the ball into my chest, walking away.

Well that fucking sucked.

I haven't talked to Rave in a couple of weeks. She's been avoiding my damn texts and calls. From overhearing my parents talk, her parents are worried. I know she's probably hanging out with that guy she's dating tonight so I'm going to troll around until I find them. My hometown, Everly, is only a couple of towns over from Greenville where she lives. I've gone out with a couple of girls from over there and I have a couple of guy friends so I kinda know their local hangouts. I pull into the Texaco parking lot where there are several trucks backed up with people sitting on the tailgates. I see her off to the side talking with who I'm assuming is the guy she's dating. Parking my truck, I think about how glad I am I got my license at the start of summer. Sitting at home or asking for rides would suck. I immediately see Cher, one of the girls I went out with from over here. "Hey, sweetie. How are you?"

She gives me a smile. "Good. What about you?"

"Doin' all right. Enjoying summer." She and I ended things on good terms. At the time, neither of us could drive so seeing each other was kind of hard. We just went our separate ways.

She leans into me. "I don't mean to get in your girl's business, but she needs to be careful of Shane. He's got a reputation for being kind of extreme." Everyone knows that Rave and I are best friends, so her telling me this means something.

I nod. "Yeah. She's gotten into some trouble over him already."

"He's just—Watch out for her."

"Okay. Thanks for the heads up." I walk toward Raven and this guy. She looks up to see me and where normally she'd have a smile on her face, she looks like she's dreading it.

"Rave, what's going on?" I ask casually.

"Um, not much. What are you doing here?" she says with some nervousness.

"Rode over to hang with some of the people I know. Not much going on in Everly. Cher and I used to date, thought I'd come see what's going on," I explain and then stick my hand out to the guy. "Grant Hudson, nice to meet you."

He begrudgingly shakes my hand. "Shane Gibson, Raven's boyfriend."

I laugh. "Yeah, I kinda gathered that."

He cocks his head to the side. "So you here to rat her out to her parents for being with me?"

I look to Raven and then back to him. "No, man, like I said, I'm just here to hang out. Thought I'd come over and speak. Why, is she not supposed to be hanging out with you or something?"

"Her parents are just a little uptight. They don't see how much she means to me. These other guys don't see her like I do. They just see a tomboy, muscles and all. I see something else. Something with potential." He pulls her closer into his side. "Isn't that right, babe?" She looks up at him with a smile that doesn't quite reach her eyes.

Wait, did he just put her down and then try to make a compliment out of it? I need to walk away from here before I lose my shit.

"Okay, well I'm gonna go catch up over here. I'll talk to you guys later."

I talk with some of the people I know and cut up, watching her out of the corner of my eye all night. Soon, I see them load up in his truck and leave.

One of the guys from their basketball team that I'm friends with looks at me. "Dude, she's in over her head with him. Several of us tried to talk to her after they went out the first time, but she's not listening." The only thing I can do is shake my head.

An hour later, I've decided she's not coming back, so I start driving back to Everly. As I'm turning off highway 301, my phone rings. Glancing at the screen, I see it's Rave.

"Hey, Rave. What's up?"

"Um, are you already headed back home?"

"Yeah, but I'm not far. Why?"

"I need a ride."

"You need a ride? Where is the guy you are dating?" I'm getting a little pissed now, but I'm already turning the truck around.

I hear a catch in her voice. "Never mind."

"Rave, wait. Where are you? I'm already headed back your way."

She mumbles, telling me she's in the Hardee's parking lot. It only takes me about five minutes to get to her. She climbs into the truck as soon as I stop. Her hair is down now and she's quiet.

Before I ever back out of the spot, I turn to her. "What in the fuck is going on?"

She jumps a little at my raised voice. "Nothing, we just had an argument and I said I'd find another way home."

I can tell she's rattled. "Okay." I figure simple is better right now. Maybe when she comes over with her parents tomorrow, I can get her to talk.

Pulling into her driveway, she looks over at me with sad eyes. "I'll see you tomorrow. Thanks for the ride, but please keep it to yourself."

I nod. "Okay. No problem."

We are out on my driveway playing some one-on-one. She's in a pair of shorts and a long-sleeved shirt with her hair down. As I go to reach in, I end up with a handful of hair. "Ouch. Shit, Grant."

"Sorry. Why do you have your damn hair down anyway? You know better than that," I say in a huff, walking around. "While we are at it, it's like ninety damn degrees out here. Why are you in long sleeves?"

She backs away from me. "Just shut up and leave me alone. It's none of your business."

I follow her and pretty much trap her by our garage. She has this panicked look on her face. I hate that she has that. Pulling her hair up, I see a handprint on her neck. I shove her sleeves up and see another hand print on her opposite arm. "What in the hell, Rave? Did he do this to you last night?"

She shoves me in the chest. "Just shut up. You don't know anything."

"I know he put his fucking hands on you. You didn't do that to yourself!"

I don't realize how bad our voices are raised until my mom, Anne, speaks. "What are you two doing?"

I spin around and we both start spouting off at the same time. My mom throws her hand up to silence us, just like she did when we were kids. "Stop. Come inside, both of you."

Once we are inside, her parents look at us. Her dad, Warren, speaks first, "Now, do you two wanna tell us what in the hell is going on?"

Raven crosses her arms over her chest, so I speak. "I had to pick her up last night after she and that douche she's dating had it out. She told me it was just an argument and she decided to find another way home, but the bruises she's sporting today tell me a different story."

She looks at me with anger and betrayal. "Go to hell, Grant!"

Her mom, Tara's, face looks like she just got punched. "Raven Anne Quinn! Watch your language."

Warren steps forward. "Where are the bruises?"

Raven refuses to speak. My dad, Greg, looks fucking pissed. Finally, I speak. "Her neck and arm. It looks like a handprint."

Her dad pulls her hair out of the way and I hear a gasp from her mom and mine.

Warren looks at me. "Why didn't you tell us last night you had to bring her home?"

I sigh. "She asked me not to. But today I saw the bruises. She needs to stay away from him. Plus, he talked about you like you were shit in front of me last night."

"Shut up, Grant! You don't know anything about him! None of you do! Don't sit in judgment over him. He has no one but me. I did tell him to leave me, that I'd find another way home! The hand marks were an accident."

"An accident?!" her dad yells. "How exactly does someone grab you hard enough to cause bruising?"

Tara steps in the middle of all of us. "Let's calm down. Sit down, Raven, we need to talk."

"What, so you can all gang up on me? Tell me how the one guy who finds me attractive is bad for me? Why don't you talk to Grant about banging half of the girls he goes to school with?" she yells.

My parents glare at me in a look that says we'll talk later. Fuck, she had to drag my sex life into this. What of it there is. She acts like I'm a whore or something. Yes, I've slept with a few girls, but not that damn many.

Her mother stops her. "This isn't about Grant. He isn't coming home with bruises from one of those floozies." Now they are floozies. Where are these floozies? "This is about you, so park your happy ass on one of those stools, missy."

Raven slumps into one of the stools around my parents' island. Normally most people would think this situation is weird and that her parents would leave our house instead of arguing in front of us. But not our parents. Our dads were frat brothers and our mothers were sorority sisters. My dad is closer to Warren than he is his own brother and her mom, Tara, has nothing to do with her family, so in their mind we're one big happy family.

After everyone is seated around the bar, Tara looks at her. "Raven, we've decided that you're moving to Everly this year." Raven goes to argue but her mom puts her hand up. "Stop. I feel like you need to get away from this boy. School starts back in two weeks. This summer has been a dramatic rollercoaster. I've watched you withdraw from life. You've gotten into more trouble than ever before. Your phone bill is crazy with how much he calls and texts. You're arguing with us every day. We just can't keep doing things this way. You know plenty of people at Everly, plus Grant is there." Raven looks at me like she's going to set me on fire.

"How will I get to school?"

"The first two weeks one of us will drive you, after that you'll have your license. You know we've already found you a small car to drive so you can drive to school. If we find out you're seeing him, though, you'll lose the car and we'll keep driving you to school." Her mom shakes her head and looks to her dad.

Warren speaks up. "This is serious, Raven. I want to beat the hell out of that kid right now. I was up in the air about the school decision until tonight. If I find out you're seeing him or talking to him, you'll think prison would be a nice vacation."

My mom steps forward and pulls Raven into a forced hug. "Raven, baby, you're scaring all of us. I also don't know why you think this boy is the only one who thinks you're attractive. I see a beautiful girl."

"Thank you, Anne, but that's easy for you to say. You aren't built like a damn giant," she says with an angry sob.

My mom looks at me. "Grant, why don't you, your dad and Warren go outside and shoot a round? I think we need some girl time in here."

My dad persuades Warren and me to follow him outside. Dad levels his eyes at Warren. "Warren, Rave's gonna be fine. It's high school, you put some distance between her and that kid, it'll get better."

Warren nods. "I know, but the idea that he had enough balls to put his hands on her..."

Finally, my dad, wanting to break the tension, looks at me. "So what's this about *your* extracurricular activities?"

The look on my face must say a lot because Warren actually is able to laugh at me. My dad shakes his head. "Dad, it's not as bad as Rave made it out. Hell, you see how busy I stay with practice and crap, I don't have a lot of time."

Warren chuckles, "Don't worry, son. You probably don't need a lot of time right now, that's something you learn."

Oh my God, I'm going to die.

My dad shakes his head, looking up at the sky. "Just tell me you're being smart. I'm way too damn young to be a grandfather."

I shrug and kick at the ground. Fuck, this is embarrassing. "Yes, Dad. The few times, yes. I'm stressing the *few* times."

Jesus, I'm going to kill Rave. She just threw me to the damn lions.

CHAPTER 3

Raven-

Grant Hudson is a fucking asshole. After an hour of listening to his mom and mine try to convince me that I'm beautiful, I was ready to run out in traffic. So I just finally agreed. I was beyond exhausted and ready to go home. After I had my parents convinced that I was ready to leave Shane behind and move on to a new school, they finally decided we could go home. Grant has tried to call me like fifteen times since the other night, but I'm not talking to him. I'll end up having to talk to him at school, but I want that to be as little as possible, too.

My phone was confiscated for a few days by my dad. He read every text that came from Shane, some that were pretty embarrassing for me and raised my dad's blood pressure through the roof. He never responded to them, though, then Shane made the mistake of calling. My dad pretty much informed him that if he found out he was coming near me again, he didn't mind going to jail for beating the shit out of him. Then several of my team members figured out my parents were moving me and although they were upset about losing me to an opposing team, a couple of them said they thought me getting away from Shane was the smarter move. I don't understand how this became everyone's business. None of them know Shane like I do. They don't understand the stress he's under, what it's like to have no one, not even your own parents care about you. He needs my love; he knows I'm the only person that truly cares about him. It's becoming clear to me that he's possibly the only person who really cares about my feelings, too. I don't get what everyone has against us.

I miss him. Even when he was a jerk, he's really the only person who knew me. He loved all the parts of my body, even the ones others thought were too much like a boy. Well, he likes them enough to want me. He still wishes my boobs were bigger, but he was pretty patient with me about the sex thing. I mean he waited several weeks for me to finally give it up.

So now I sit here at breakfast with my parents before my first day at Everly High. My eggs and grits just don't seem that appetizing right now. Some people call them butterflies in your stomach when you're nervous, I'd call them bats. There are a whole flock of them going around and around in my stomach.

"Sweetie, you need to eat," my mom says, drawing my attention back to the table.

I shrug. "I'm just not that hungry. I'm really nervous."

My dad shrugs. "Nothing to be nervous about. You know some people from Everly, you'll be fine." He shoves his empty plate forward. "Plus, you'll have Grant."

I roll my eyes. Why does everyone feel the need to point out that I'll have Grant? I don't want Grant right now. The only thing I want to do with Grant is kick his fucking ass.

"At least eat your toast, sweetie," my mom pleads.

Trying to make her happy, I nab the toast at the edge of my plate and munch on it while drinking some orange juice. Grabbing my backpack and my gym bag, I follow my dad out to his truck. We went last week to set up my classes. The basketball coach tells me I'll have to try out, but he's seen me play and knows that I would be an asset to his team. It also helps that his shooting guard graduated last year, so he needs one. I've played shooting guard and point guard for years, so I have some playing experience. Since most of the high schools in this county are sixth through twelfth, most people start playing Junior Varsity in seventh or eighth grade, instead of ninth like bigger places. So I have quite a bit of playing time against bigger and more experienced opponents. In turn, I have two P.E. classes. One that's specifically for athletes and weight training, while the other one is just a gym class. That is nice since my old school didn't offer that.

As we pull into the school parking lot, my dad looks over at me. "Rave, I really do hope you have a good day. In the end, I hope you realize this is for the best."

I hoist up my bags as I prepare to get out. "Yeah, Dad."

I see him shake his head. "Your mom will be here to get you after school. Coach said that you guys won't start practice for tryouts for another couple of weeks."

"Okay, thanks." I shut the truck door and make my way into the entrance of the school. Finding the locker they assigned me the other day, I open it and store some of my supplies.

"Hey, are you new?" I turn to see a pretty blonde girl.

"Yes, today is my first day," I respond.

She sticks her hand out. "I'm Vivian."

"Raven, nice to meet you."

"Do you have your schedule yet?"

I pull the piece of paper out from my backpack that the lady in guidance gave me when I registered. "Yeah, I got it the other day when they enrolled me."

She looks over the paper. "Oh, we have Mr. Carnley's class together and a gym class."

"Which gym glass?" I ask. She's tall, she could be on the basketball team, but I don't remember her.

"Seventh period."

"What sport do you play?"

"I'm a cheerleader." Well, that fits, too. "And I run cross country in the spring." Okay, so she does something other than cheer.

"Not all of the cheerleaders do the seventh period gym, but I'm a base so I need the weight training, plus it helps with my running," she explains.

"Hey, Viv," I hear behind me.

I turn to see another girl. She's in relaxed clothes and she's carrying a big ass book bag. "Hey, Joelle. This is Raven, she's new."

The other girl, now known as Joelle, raises her full hands. "Hey, my friends call me Jo. Welcome to the shitty halls of Everly High."

I have to laugh; she seems like a smartass after my own heart.

"Raven is in Mr. Carnley's class with us."

Jo nods. "Great, he's pretty funny in an *I'm a dork* sort of way."

"Thanks. Do you have seventh period gym as well?"

She swaps out some books in her locker. "No, that's for the jocks. My brother is in there since he's a football player. I'm in band that period."

"Oh, okay," I answer as she takes my schedule from my hand.

"Oh, well we do have study hall together with Coach Fagan and you have English with my friend Clem."

"Did I hear my name?" a girl says over her shoulder.

"Yeah, this is Raven, she's new." She goes over what they've figured out about my schedule.

Clem steps up. "So what sport do you play? Since, you know, you're in that gym class."

"I play basketball."

They all nod. Clem speaks up again. "I'm in band right now, but I play softball in the spring. So I'll be switching at the end of first semester to that gym class."

I smile. "Awesome." Okay, so it seems these girls may be okay.

"Well, what do we have here?" a snarky voice comes from behind me.

I see Vivian shy away a little before she speaks. "Ciara, this is Raven, she's new."

I see the girl look me over before sticking her nose in the air and walking on with two peons behind her.

Vivian gives me a soft smile as the trio walks away. "You'll have to excuse Ciara—"

"She's a bitch," she's cut off by Jo.

Clem nods. "She really is. I mean Viv here is a cheerleader, but I don't feel like holding her head underwater every time I see her. Ciara's I do. Not to mention her little side bitches."

Jo laughs. "I call them the queen Bs. Just don't let them bug you. Most everyone else is cool here. Ciara's lifelong dream is to fuck her way into a penthouse or the mayor's mansion. So any female here she sees as competition."

I snort. "Sorry. I like you. You're a smart ass and that I get."

"So do you know anyone else here?" Clem asks.

"I know a couple of the girls on the basketball team because I came from Greenville, so we've played each other and been to some of the same camps. I grew up with Grant Hudson, so I know a couple of the guys from his team, too," I explain.

Clem starts laughing. "Grant. You grew up with Grant?"

"Yeah, trust me, he's a pain in the ass." I roll my shoulders.

She shakes her head. "Oh, I don't mean that. Grant is one of the guys Ciara has her eye on."

"So, it's not like that with us. He's on my shit list right now anyway. He's the reason I'm here."

Clem and Jo both form an O with their mouths while Vivian stands there quietly. The bell rings, rescuing me from the next question. “Thanks for getting to know me, guys. It’s nice to know some people going into classes.”

They all smile and Jo grabs my arm. “Come on, I’ll show you to our study hall.”

As we enter the door, we’re met by a shorter man with grey hair. “Prescott.” He nods at Joelle.

“He’s Coach Fagan, he calls everyone by their last name. He’s the head football coach and also over the jock gym class.”

“Prescott. Why must you call it the jock gym class?” the old man says, startling both of us.

She turns to him with her hand on her hip. “Because that’s what it is. Duh.”

He laughs. “Okay, so it is.” He looks to me, “And you are?”

I smile. “Raven Quinn.”

He nods with recognition. “Ah, Coach O said he had a new ringer coming in.”

“He told me I’d still have to try out, but that he felt good about it.”

Coach laughs. “Yeah, well I remember seeing you play against us last year, so I’d say we feel pretty good about it.” He motions to the room. “Seats are open, just pick one and work on something quietly.”

I see that Joelle has already taken a seat in the back corner of the room. She’s taking out a computer to work on. I take a seat a couple up from her. Good thing I brought a book to read.

CHAPTER 4

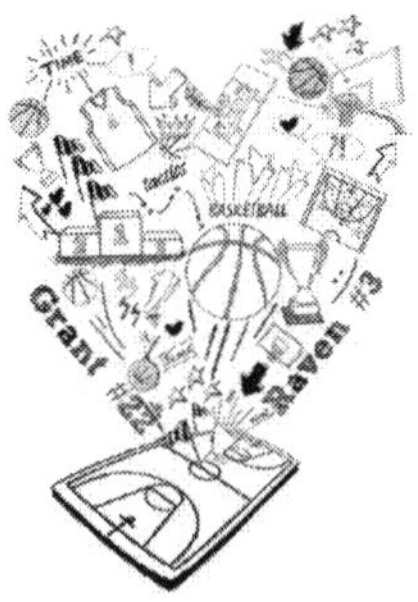

Grant-

I haven't seen Raven all day, but I'm sure I'll see her during gym. She's been avoiding me since the showdown at my parents. Which, thanks to her, ended up with my mom grilling me about my sex life. Well, like I told them, what little there is of it. Raven made it seem like I had an endless damn line of girls in and out of my bed, when in reality I've had two—one of the girls I dated for like a year and the other one was a stupid mistake. Although, I did overhear my parents talking about some damn explicit text that asshole sent her and Warren read it. That fucker *is* dumb; Warren is going to end up in jail for killing that guy. Raven gets her height from her dad. He's a big mother fucker. I'm six-one, Rave is five-nine, he makes us both look like midgets. It's funny to see her parents beside each other because her mom is only like five-four.

It's been the typical first day of school other than that. Ciara has decided that her plays this semester will be for Collin Atwood. No shocker there, she's a chick on a power trip and he's our star quarterback, and no doubt one day he could be a pro player. He's a cool guy, though. Yeah, she's flirted with me a lot through the years, but personally I think she's a bitch. I've pretty much let her know that, too, so she stays clear of me. Her little protégé, on the other hand, Karmen, has told me more than once the things she'd like to do alone with me. I don't trust her either.

Finally, the lunch bell rings and I truck it to the cafeteria. The first day of school is always taco day and for some reason, our tacos are awesome. The rest of the food is hit or miss, but I can always count on the tacos.

As I enter the cafeteria, it's a mad house. I see all of my fellow athletes are lined up. Once I'm in line, I see her sitting across the room eating with Jo and Clem. That's good, I know she's made a couple of good girlfriends.

Collin gets in line behind me. "Hey, man. Always look forward to tacos on the first day of school."

"Yep. How's practice been going? Ready for the season to start?"

He lets out a huge sigh. "Yeah, just a lot more pressure this year. You know?"

I nod. "Tell me about it, Coach is really talking about me playing point guard this year and it was one thing to play it sometimes in J.V., but in Varsity it's another thing completely."

"So you're gonna be QB on the court. Good to know. I've been freaking stressing about it. It seems like every damn corner I turn, there's some old guy telling me that the town is relying on me to get that State title." He rubs his head. "Sometimes I just wonder if it's all worth it."

I put my hand on his shoulder. "You can do it, man. We're just going to have to rely on each other."

"Do I need to break out the tissues for you two crybabies?" Dallas Kent, one of the other football players, says behind Collin. "It seems to me you both have sand in your girly parts or something."

We both tell him to shut up as we fix our trays. Once I'm back in the dining area, I find her table and go that way. I slide into the bench beside her. "Hey, how's the first day been?"

She looks over to the left at me, clearly annoyed. "Fine."

I glance to Clem and Jo. "Hey, ladies."

The both nod and say hello to acknowledge me.

All too soon, Karmen is at my side. “Hey, Grant. I’ve missed you so much this summer.”

I see Raven and the other girls roll their eyes. “Yeah, Karmen. How was your summer?”

“Good. I spent some time in the sun. I’d be happy to show you my tan lines later.” And she winks. Actually fucking winks.

But leave it to Jo to save the day. “Karmen, are you all right? Are you having some kind of seizure? I mean your eye is fluttering and stuff.”

I can’t help but start laughing, which in turn causes Karmen to throw a serious bitch face to Jo. But Jo’s cool, she just shrugs it off. As Karmen storms away, everyone starts laughing. Jo looks around, “What? I thought she needed medical help.”

“Thanks, Jo. She will just not get a freaking clue.”

Clem looks at me with a duh look. “Well, if you hadn’t banged her BFF, maybe she wouldn’t be trying to follow in her footsteps. You know, trying to see if you live up to the hype and all.”

Jo nods. I look over at Raven and cringe when I see the disgusted look on her face.

“Hey, that was a mistake I made *once* and I’ll never do it again,” I explain, hoping to remove Raven’s pissed off face, but it still fails.

As the bell rings letting us know lunch is over, I grab her tray. “I’ll see you in gym?”

She just gives me a quick nod. “Thanks for taking that.” She points to the tray before she walks out.

She’s been at this school a damn month and still doing a fairly decent job of ignoring me. She’s made the girls’ basketball team, so I see her as our practices overlap and we have a gym class. But that’s all.

That’s how I find myself sitting on the hood of her car waiting for her practice to finish up. We’ve been friends too long to let some asshole ex-boyfriend come between us.

My teammate, Preston, walks out of the gym and stops. "So, you and the new girl, huh?"

"It's not like that with us. She and I have been friends since birth. Our parents are close." I shrug.

"So you're saying she's available?"

"I don't know. I don't think she's dating anyone." I'm not privy to her private life anymore.

"You think you could hook me up with her?" he asks with a grin. "She's pretty hot."

"Fuck no, I'm not hooking you up with my best friend. Why would I do that, ass face?"

"Because we're teammates and you're a team player," he says frankly.

"Yeah, well you're just a player, no team play on this."

As she walks out of the gym, I see her talking to Crystal, a senior and the captain of her team. Good, she's not even paying attention to me sitting here.

Preston tips his chin up. "Ladies, lookin' lovely. If you ever need an extra hand in the shower after practice, I'd be happy to help." Jeez, he is such a damn flirt.

Crystal rolls her eyes. "Cut the shit, Preston."

He holds his hand to his chest. "You wound me, Crys. This is just the kind of friend I am."

She shoves him and starts to walk away, waving at us. He follows her, making some comment about her ass. He's such a little shit, but a great friend.

Raven finishes approaching the car and ignores me while she opens the car door, throwing her gym bag in the passenger seat. When I don't make a move, she stops in front of me, putting her hands on her hips with attitude. "What do you want, Grant?"

I slide off the car, standing beside it. "We need to talk." I step toward her. "I'm tired of you ignoring me. We've been friends too long for this bullshit. You're my best friend and I thought that meant something to you."

She sighs, shaking her head. "I was really pissed, okay? You brought all of this attention to nothing. Nothing. I had to change schools, break up with my boyfriend and be grounded, all because you misunderstood something."

She still doesn't see this guy for who he is. "Let me ask you a question about this Shane guy. Did he ever try to come make it right with your parents? If this was truly a misunderstanding and I were him, I'd try to get your parents to understand."

"No and I've explained this to them. He doesn't understand what it's like to have good parents, his don't care. Therefore, he doesn't get that my parents are only worried about me."

"He should respect you enough to want to explain it, though. I'm sorry, my opinion is that you dodged a bullet. He talked down to you in front of me. I had to pick you up. You are my best friend and you could've been in danger and that's how I see it." I put my hand on her shoulder. "We need to get past this. I'm worried about you."

She shakes her head. "I'm fine. I've made friends here. I can't see Shane, but other than that I'm doing okay."

"I want us to be cool. I want to shoot a round and not feel this damn pressure. Hell, I could be pissed with you, too. You made it seem like I'm the biggest male whore in school. My mom reamed my ass."

She laughs. "Well, you are."

"No, I'm not. I've had sex with two people. Yes, I've fooled around a little with some other girls, but I've had sex with Tabitha, who I dated for a damn year, and I fucked up one night and had sex with Satan's princess, Ciara. I regret that, mainly because I can't stand her."

Rave throws her hands in the air. "Well, then why in the hell would you do it with her?"

I let out a long breath. "I was in a bad place after my break up with Tabby. I thought I'd use that old adage about getting over someone and I was drunk and she was willing. I guess I was drunk enough to drown out how annoying she is. Anyway, it was stupid and I regret it."

I see that her posture has finally relaxed a little. "Okay. Sorry I made it out to your parents and mine that you were a whore."

"So are you going to actually speak to me at my parents' house this weekend? Because last weekend at yours just got freakin' awkward."

Finally, she nods. "Yeah, we'll play some one-on-one." She motions to her car. "Can I go now?"

I laugh. "Yeah, go home."

CHAPTER 5

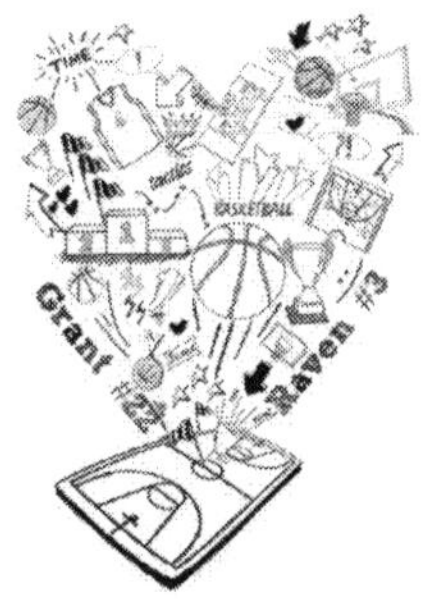

Raven-

So moving to Everly hasn't been too bad. I have a few friends, the girls I'm playing with seem to appreciate my skill more and I feel like I mesh better with this team. Per my parents' request, I haven't seen Shane, but I have slipped a few phone calls to him. He misses me and we plan to meet up this weekend. I'm going to have to be slick about getting out and I have to make sure wherever we go, Grant doesn't see us.

"Hey, Rave, how's it going?" I turn to see a smiling Jo.

She's been happier lately, it must be the guy in her life. Although last week was a bit hectic for her. Her dad had a heart attack. He just got to come home a day or so ago.

"Not much. Just glad to be closing in on the weekend. You'll have Friday night off, won't you? Since it's a bye week?"

She grins. "Yes, and I have a date that night."

"Oh. Well, that sounds good. I heard there is a party at the Daffin's place both nights. Do you think you'll go?" I ask.

She shakes her head. "No, I don't want to. Booker Daffin gets on my nerves and I don't trust him."

"Okay. I might go out there one night. I'm sure I'll see your brother there," I say with a laugh. Since I started here, I've met her brother, James, and he's pretty funny. I also think there is something going on between him and Clem, but neither will tell Jo. But then Clem has some weird relationship with one of the guys on the baseball team, Harrison. So I'm not sure what to make of all of it. She swears she and Harrison are just friends, but the way he looks at her sometimes gets me turned on, and I'm only watching.

She chuckles. "I'm sure you will, he never likes to miss a party. I'm just not big on hanging out there, you know?"

"Yeah, I didn't figure that a lot would change about you just because you started dating Collin." I laugh. "I mean we can only have one Ciara in this place, you know?"

She snorts. "You're coming along nicely, Rave. I have you lured to my side."

"No, I just know a bitch when I see one." Plus, it pisses me off for some reason that she slept with Grant and that her best friend is trying to jump on his dick every chance she gets. Girls like that annoy the hell out of me.

She closes her locker. "Good eye." She adjusts her backpack on her shoulder. "Well, I'll see you later. I gotta get to Home Ec."

I throw up my hand. "See you."

After school, I make the excuse to my dad that I need *feminine* products from Wal-Mart, so I can get up with Shane about this weekend. My dad is awesome but you start talking about tampons or pads and he gets squeamish and tries to get off the phone. I know I have at least an hour buffer before he'll expect me home.

I called Shane earlier today about meeting me on a cheap disposable phone I bought a week ago. This way my parents can't monitor my contact with him. I wait in the parking lot at the Wal-Mart complex for him. He's late. Once he finally pulls in beside me, he motions for me to get in his truck. Grabbing my keys, I lock up my car and jump in his truck.

He doesn't say a word to start with, he quickly backs out of the parking spot and starts down the road.

I break the silence. "Hey."

He looks at me and grins, "Hey, babe."

I look around, wondering where we're going. He knows I don't have long. "So where are we off to?"

"Just down the street," he says, glancing at me.

"Okay, I just gotta keep track of time if I don't want to get in trouble. That way we can meet up this weekend."

He nods. "Yeah, I know."

He pulls into a two-trail road that leads down by the river. Once he parks the truck, he looks at me, grabbing my arm to pull me over to him.

As soon as I'm in his lap, he's grabbing my shirt to pull it over my head. "Wait," I breathe out as he nips at my neck.

"Babe," he sighs, "we don't have much time and I need you. I've missed you. Do you know how long it's been for me? This is the longest I've ever been without sex."

"I just thought we'd get to catch up."

He dismisses me. "We'll do that this weekend when we have more time. Right now, I need to be inside you."

Finally, I nod as he finishes pulling my shirt over my head. Twenty minutes later, I'm already dressed and we're heading back to my car.

Once we arrive at my car, he looks over at me. "I'll get up with you about this weekend. I'm gonna be kinda busy, but we'll figure it out. You'll just need to be available when I call."

That's all he has to say. "Um, okay."

"You better get whatever you're supposed to be picking up so you don't get busted. I wanna see you. I need to see you."

I nod, getting out of the truck and walking toward the store. Once I'm inside, I find the nearest bathroom and cry. I know he misses me, but I feel like there is this wedge between us. It's my fault for not being there for him now. He's at a school where everyone treats him like a criminal. I'm sure the girls who were using him in bed are pissed because he's no longer providing that service. I just need to make sure I'm there for him this weekend.

The week goes by and I hear nothing. I know there's a party going on tonight and tomorrow, but I sit at home and wait for him to call me. Which he never does. I guess he'll call me tonight.

Around five, my mom sticks her head in my room. "Hey, I have a surprise for you."

I look up from my kindle. "Yeah?"

"I know this year has been a big adjustment. You've done great at Everly so you, me and Anne are going to get manicures and pedicures. I know yours probably need to be trimmed and shaped, so let's go," she says with a huge smile. I can't say this is out of the ordinary, we normally do this before my season starts. Long or unshaped nails and basketball don't mix.

I glance at my bag, thinking about the phone I'm not supposed to have. I still haven't heard from him. "Now?" I don't want to wait on his call anymore, but he'll feel rejected and pissed if I don't.

She grins. "Yeah, now. We're going to that new place in Monroe. *The Nail Bar*."

"Um, Mom...I can't drink."

She laughs. "Yes, I know this, but Anne and I can. You get to be our designated driver. Plus, it'll be fun. I want to do something fun with you. I figure there, you should see some entertainment."

"What do you mean?" I ask, genuinely curious.

"Well, let's just say I heard that last week Reverend Tempt's wife got a little heavy handed with her wine and started telling everyone how lousy he was in bed. And all about a few of the members who got some cosmetic enhancements done. Sounds like a ton of fun," she says, giggling like she's back in school. She may have already been into some wine.

"What does Dad say about this?"

She grins. "He's having a boys' night with Greg. One of their old frat brothers is here so they're doing their own thing."

I snicker. "So you and Anne decided that you wanna go get tipsy and get your nails done?" Figuring he won't call until way later anyway, I nod, smiling, and grab my flip flops. "Let's go."

I'm the first one finished getting my nails done. I only do clear polish on my hands and I have to keep them super short for ball so it doesn't take long. Also, Mom and Anne are enjoying the bar part.

"Mom, I'm going to go next door and grab a sub, I'll grab you both one." I know they'll need something to sober up a little.

She gives me a really big smile. "Okay, sweetie. Here, take some money." She hands me a couple of twenties. "Grab us some chips, too."

Anne perks up. "Ooh! Doritos if they have them."

I give them both a little laugh. "Okay, I'll be back."

I go next door to the sub shop and place our order. Within a few minutes, I have our subs, their chips and me a bottle of water.

Walking out the door, I hear someone squeal. I look in the direction of the noise and see Shane with some brunette girl. He has her pinned against the side of his truck and she has her legs wrapped around him while he kisses her neck.

So that's the plans he had this weekend. So much for him not having sex. Pulling the phone from my purse, I text him.

ME: Why haven't you called me?

I watch him pull the phone from his pocket and read my text. Soon, my phone buzzes.

SHANE: Sorry babe. Been wrapped up with work today. I'm exhausted. I'm gonna go home and crash. Hopefully tomorrow night will work better. I miss you. Can't wait to feel your body against mine again.

Huh. That asshole. I feel my eyes burning with tears. I can't cry. I can't. My mom will know something is going on.

ME: It appears more like you have someone wrapped around you. If that's work then you should know prostitution is still illegal.

Right before I hit send, I grab the door of the nail shop and watch him through the window.

He looks at his phone once it buzzes, pushing the girl from his waist and glares around the parking lot. He motions to the girl and they get in his truck and squeal out of the parking lot.

Grabbing my regular phone from my bag, I call Clem. She answers on the second ring.

"What's up, Rave?"

"You going to Daffin's party?"

"Not tonight, I have a family thing, but probably tomorrow night. You wanna go?"

"Yep. I'll call you tomorrow."

"What are you doing now?"

I laugh because if I don't, I'll cry. "I'm at *The Nail Bar* with my mom and Grant's mom."

"That place is so much fun. Did you hear about the Reverend's wife last week?"

I shake my head. "Yeah, my mom told me."

"It's places like that that make me wish I was older," she says with a sigh into the phone.

"Well, my mom and Anne are enjoying it, that's for sure. I'm going to have to drive them home," I say with a laugh.

She laughs loudly. "Well, I'll call you tomorrow and we'll talk about going out to Daffin's."

We say goodbye and hang up. A few hours later, I've gotten my mom and Anne home. Now I'm sitting on my bed, pissed about Shane. I can't believe I fell for all of his shit. He was basically screwing another girl in the parking lot. I haven't even checked the phone I use for him.

Pulling the phone out, I read the texts he's sent. They go from "What are you talking about?" to "It's not what you think." To "Please talk to me." To "You fucking bitch. You're a whore and a lousy fuck. If you were a good girlfriend I wouldn't need to fuck someone else."

The more I think about our relationship, the angrier I get. I send him a text.

ME: We're finished. I don't want to see you again.

SHANE: Fine! You can be like everyone else in my life and let me down. I might as well not even be alive, I should just go ahead and off myself. Not like anyone would miss me.

I think about texting him back, but that will just drag this on. He wants me to feel bad for him. Yes, his mom sucks, but that doesn't give him the right to cheat on me.

The phone keeps going off all night. He's sorry. He can't live without me. He didn't mean the things he said. He thinks he's a sex addict, that's why he screwed around on me.

Ugh! I'm going to ignore him and I'm going to that party tomorrow night. And I'm going to find the sexiest thing in my closet to go in.

Walking around with Clem, she keeps introducing me to more and more people. I guess these parties get pretty big and kids from all over the county come.

She stops, shocked, but smiles happily. "I didn't think they were coming."

I look around and know automatically who she is talking about. The cutest couple ever. Jo and Collin have arrived. Jo comes over and speaks with us briefly, but then gets sidelined by others.

I turn to walk back to the bonfire and walk straight into Grant. "Hey."

"Hey, sorry. I need to watch where I'm going."

He shrugs. "No biggie. So you had to be my mom's DD last night I heard."

I laugh. "Yeah, they got a little too tipsy getting their nails done."

He shakes his head. "Damn."

I look across the fire to see someone who doesn't need to be here. "I'll be right back."

I storm around the fire and stare at Shane. "What are you doing here?"

He growls. "What are you doing here?" He points in the direction I just came from. "And flirting with your *friend*? You were screwing him all along, weren't you?"

My face feels like it's on fire I'm so pissed. "No, you're the only person I would be STUPID enough to screw around with."

I can tell he's stunned by my anger. Normally I never argue back with him like this.

"I'm just all alone at our school now and I miss you."

My heart pangs because if I hadn't had to leave Greenville, he wouldn't be alone and we'd probably be happy.

His hand on my arm pulls me from my thoughts. "Come on, baby. Let's go to my truck and talk."

Talking was what we were supposed to do the other day, when all he wanted was a quick piece of ass. So I stump him. "So you didn't screw the girl I saw you mauling in the parking lot yesterday?"

He then grips my arm, "Let's go talk about this somewhere else."

"Problem here?" Grant appears over my shoulder.

Shane cocks his head. "No. No problem, asshole. She doesn't need you around here. Run home and tell Mommy and Daddy all about me being here."

"Shane! That was uncalled for." I turn to Grant. "I'm fine."

Grant starts to say something but I shush him. Shane tightens his grip on my arm and starts to tug me away. As we reach the edge of the crowd, I stop. “Shane, I don’t want to talk to you.”

He pulls me in for a hard kiss and I shove him away. “Fucking tease!” he yells.

I draw back and slap him across the face. After which he grabs me by my hair and tries to drag me toward his truck. I kick at him, but before I can do anything else, all hell breaks loose.

Fuck me.

CHAPTER 6

Grant-

Coming to this party was a last minute decision. I was bored and I seriously need to get laid. A lot of people from all over the county show up at these things, so maybe I can find a girl to hook up with for the night. At *least* get a blowjob. This school year has been one big dry spell. Before, I never cared, but having Raven at my school, I don't want her to think I'm some kind of douche just trying to hook up with people.

Normally I don't come out here to the Daffin farm. If I'm being honest, I can't stand Booker. I think he's a dick and his family acts like they're better than everyone. Like everyone in this town owes them something.

I'm glad to see Collin get here with his girl. I wouldn't have ever pictured them together, but they work. He sees me and motions that he's coming over, but gets stopped by some people on the way. I don't know who the girl is they're talking to. Her back is to me. She has on some of those damn jeans that are sparkled or something and her ass really fills them out. The back of the shirt she's wearing hangs open; whoever this girl is isn't wearing a bra and her fucking hair. Holy shit, that hair. I need to go introduce myself, see if the front matches the back and see if I can talk that sexy fucking creature into following me to my truck.

Walking toward Collin, I almost trip over my feet when the girl turns around and I see it's Raven. HOLY SHIT.

Fuck, what's she doing here and why in the hell is she dressed like that? My body can't decide what the hell it wants to do. Go over there and tell her, my best friend, to get some damn clothes on or no, I can't even comprehend the other and I'm pissed because my crotch isn't getting the memo.

I need another fucking beer.

I grab another beer from the keg and do my best to look elsewhere. I chug that beer and the next one.

I notice her laughing with Joelle and Clem. When in the hell did she get so damn sexy? Where did those tits come from? They aren't there when we play basketball.

I turn back around from tossing my cup into the fire and Raven runs into me. "Hey," I say, touching her shoulders to help steady her.

She brushes her hair behind her ear. "Hey, sorry. I need to watch where I'm going."

Damn it, these jeans are getting uncomfortable. I need to break this tension. "No biggie. So you had to be my mom's DD last night I heard."

Thank God, she laughs. "Yeah, they got a little too tipsy getting their nails done."

"Damn." I'm shaking my head like a damn idiot.

She looks across the fire and mumbles back to me. "I'll be right back."

Great, she's trying to get away from me. I've made an ass out of myself with my best friend. I need to go. As I turn to walk away, I hear her raised voice. "What are you doing here?"

I look over there to see that asshole, Shane. I can see them having a heated discussion. I overhear her saying something about him screwing someone else. I can see in his face he's getting pissed at her and for once, I see her standing up for herself.

I start that way to see if she needs me when I hear him try to pull her away to go "talk" somewhere else.

"Problem here?" I say as I walk up behind her.

Shane cocks his head. "No. No problem, asshole. She doesn't need you around here. Run home and tell Mommy and Daddy all about me being here."

"Shane! That was uncalled for," she shouts at him and then turns to me. "I'm fine."

I start to stay something but she shuts me up with a death glare. Fine, fuck it, she can deal with it herself. The guy takes her by the arm, pulling her away, but just as she gets to the edge of the crowd I hear her, "Shane, I don't want to talk to you."

I see him try to shove his tongue down her throat and she shoves him away. "Fucking tease!" he yells.

She slaps the shit out of his face and I'm kind of proud until she turns to come back and he grabs her by her hair, trying to drag her away.

I see red. No one has the right to touch her like that. I'm on top of him, punching him repeatedly in the face. I can hear her screaming at me, but no way am I stopping. I feel a set of strong arms pulling me away. "Whoa, Grant, buddy, stop." Just as I'm about to clock whoever is pulling me away, I look over my shoulder to see it's Collin.

Just as I'm pulled away, I get slapped in the face. "Are you fucking stupid, Grant?" Raven screams.

"Rave, he had no business putting his hands on you like that! What in the hell is he even doing here?!" I yell.

Throwing her hands in the air, she announces, "Fuck this, I'm leaving." She storms off.

"Man, what in the hell is going on? Was that your girl?" Collin asks.

I shake my head, wiping a little blood from my lip. "Raven, she's the new shooting guard on the girls' team. But she's been my best friend since we were little. She grew up in

Greenville. That's the jackass her parents have been trying to keep her away from."

"What did he do?" he asks.

"Over the summer, he roughed her up a little, upset her, and she called me. Then I talked to her parents. That really pissed her off, but someone needed to know."

He nods in understanding. "Very true, man."

James comes walking up. "Got that guy on the road, Booker told his ass to never come back." He looks around, asking Collin, "Have you seen my sister?"

I motion to them that I'm out and start walking toward my truck. I see Raven's car leaving with a cloud of dust behind it.

Fuck, I gotta fix this. I follow her as she swings into a parking lot. She needs to settle the fuck down before she gets in a wreck or gets a damn DUI. I know she didn't drink much, but we're underage.

I snatch the passenger side door open to her car and she jumps. "Are you fucking nuts? You could've gotten stopped by a cop."

"Shut the fuck up, Grant. I don't need you fucking chaperoning me. I really don't need you trying to beat people up for me either!" she says through sobs.

I slide into the small car. "I just couldn't watch him snatch you around and do nothing! It's not right, you don't deserve to be treated that way. Look, I don't mean to be an asshole, I just can't let it happen."

"Just go ahead and tell me how stupid I am and then leave," she says as she wipes tears.

"I don't see that you're stupid, I just think you fell for the wrong guy." I look around, uncomfortable; this is about to be the oddest conversation we've ever had. "So he screwed around? I didn't think you were seeing him, so how could it be considered screwing around?"

She slumps back in the seat of the car, her sobs slowing down. "We'd started sneaking around seeing each other. We were supposed to meet up this weekend, he told me he was busy yesterday. I saw him with a girl in the parking lot when I was at the nail place."

"Oh." I want to be pissed that she was still seeing him, but I can tell she's hurting. She's my friend. "I'm going to ask you a question I know is none of my business, but as your friend I need to ask it."

She rolls her eyes, "Fine."

"I'm just going to assume you were having sex with him, please tell me you were careful. If he was screwing around yesterday, he could've been the entire time."

She nods. "Yeah, I never told him I was on birth control. I didn't want him to have an excuse not to use a condom. I couldn't imagine my pills failing and me having to tell my parents that I was pregnant." She leans forward, resting her head on the steering wheel with a moan.

She's on birth control? What the hell? "Yeah, that wouldn't have been good." I swallow. "So are you going to stay away from him now?" I want to comfort her, but I'm not sure how I should do that. This conversation has gotten extremely fucking awkward.

She falls back against the seat, covering her eyes with her arm. "Yeah, I can't deal with the shit anymore. It's not worth it and I feel bad because I was all he had."

Has she lost it? "He made you think that you were all he had. He preyed on the fact that you have a good heart and would want to help him. He took advantage of you and your goodness."

She sits there staring ahead.

I reach over and pat her knee. "Are you gonna be okay to get home?"

"Yeah, I only had one beer," she explains. "So you coming over tomorrow?"

I nod. "So they tell me."

"Jeez, don't act so excited about it."

I sigh. "It's just I wish they would let us make our own plans. Just because they want to get together shouldn't mean we have to be there every time. You know?"

"Yeah, I get tired of being forced to be around you, too."

Shit, she took that wrong. "That's not what I mean. It's about them, not us."

"True. They do kind of just make us be there and don't care if we have plans," she says, laughing. "Well, I plan to make use of the pool tomorrow. It's probably the last weekend before it gets too chilly."

Her parents have a heated pool, but it can still get chilly to swim when it's cold out. "So no pickup game tomorrow then. I'll bring my swim trunks."

Her phone goes off before she can say anything.

"Holy shit. Your fight with Shane isn't the topic of conversation now," she explains.

"What do you mean?"

"Apparently, something happened with Joelle. She's at the hospital, Booker got the hell beat out of him and the cops are there." She keeps studying her phone. "Clem is texting me from the hospital."

"Do you wanna go there?"

She shakes her head. "No, she said all of us needed to stay away from there. The cops went out to the party. That's the reason she texted me to make sure we weren't still there. I guess they're taking Booker in to the police station. Whatever happened was bad."

"Do you think that shithead Shane called the cops?"

"No, from the way Clem is talking Booker did something, she said she'd call me later when she got home."

I reach for the door. "Okay, well, I'll see you tomorrow. Let me know what happened in case we need to get our stories straight."

"Yeah, okay," she says as I get out of her car.

When I arrive at her house following my parents, I go straight into her backyard after hearing the water splash from the pool.

She comes up out of the water and my mouth drops. She's in a bikini. Since we were in middle school, Raven has always worn an athletic style one-piece swimsuit. She really did get some damn boobs. Don't get me wrong, they aren't huge or anything, but they're perky for days.

I need to jump in the water or I could embarrass myself in these shorts. When did I start to notice my best friend's body? This is making my life difficult. It's got to just be a reaction to the female body. I mean it's not like I'm really attracted to her.

I bail off into the water and once I come up, she's standing in the shallow end. "Way to enter the pool, Smalls."

I push my wet hair back. "Go big or go home, you know?" I point to her suit. "So, you retire the old Nike swimsuit?"

She laughs. "Um, yeah, it got hung up in the washing machine and the straps got torn. So I bought this one a month or so ago, just haven't had the opportunity to wear it. I'll order another sports suit, though. I feel weird in this one."

I shrug, "Why? It looks great on you." Too damn great. Again, why in the hell am I noticing this?

"Really? I've never felt like my body was made for a bikini." Ugh. Now I have to tell her she really looks great in this swimsuit. I don't want her to think she doesn't look good in it. I'll sound like a jerk.

"Um, yeah. Would I lie? If you looked like crap in the thing, I'd tell you. You know this."

She shrugs. "Yeah, I guess you would tell me. You've never been shy about telling me anything." Fuck, until now.

"Just don't let Preston see you in it, okay? I don't want to have to beat his ass."

She laughs and splashes water at me. “It’s nice, the things you say about your friends.”

I splash water back. “I’m just honest. The guy is a perv. He was asking about you the other day when I was at your car.”

She shakes her head. “I think he was just being funny. I’m sure he doesn’t see me like that.”

“Um yeah, he does.” She looks at me like she needs more assurance and I can’t do that right now. So I change the subject. “So, any word on last night?”

She nods. “Come on, I’m gonna get out. Let’s go change and meet in the den.”

“Hell, I just got here.”

She shrugs. “I know, but the sun isn’t staying out so it’s getting a little cold.”

Out of habit, when girls say that I look at her boobs. Sure enough, her nipples are rock hard through her top. Shit. Yeah, I need her to go put on some big ass sweats. “Okay. I’ll be in there in a minute.” I need time for my boner to go away.

Ten minutes later, she comes in the den with a basketball shirt and gym shorts on. Thank God.

She plops down on the couch next to me and starts to speak in a hushed voice. “Okay. So apparently right after you decided to make an ass out of yourself last night, Collin couldn’t find Joelle. Someone directed him to the bathroom. When he went in, Booker had Jo up against the wall with her clothes half torn off. She was practically unconscious and that bitch Ciara was snapping pics with her phone. Long story short, Clem beat Ciara’s ass, James beat Booker’s ass, Collin took Jo to the hospital and they found out Booker had drugged her beer. The cops showed up after all of that. They arrested Booker, busted up the party and now all hell’s about to break loose apparently.” She finally takes a breath. “I just wanted to get that out before anyone came in here.”

I laugh at how her fast ramblings sounded like a girl, like a true girl. “What do you mean all hell’s about to break loose?”

"Well, I didn't know that Clem's dad is the Chief of Police, but he was part of the cops that went to bust the party up so a ton of people got into trouble, but the biggest thing is Jo is pressing charges." She relaxes back into the couch.

"She should press charges. He violated her, assaulted her." Hell, Rave really should press charges against that asshole she was involved with, but she never will.

"Well, school should be interesting tomorrow," she says with a snort. She motions to the TV, "Do you wanna watch a movie or something? Dad is finally starting the grill and our moms got into the wine. It could be a while."

Shit, our moms and wine. "Yeah, whatcha got? No chick flicks." She laughs and I level my eyes at her. "I'm serious, Rave, you're not tricking me into watching damn *Dirty Dancing* or some shit again. It's a serious knock to my manhood."

She snorts. "What manhood?"

"I could show you but then I'd have to beat you off of me," I come back and then realize how that all just sounded. "Anyway, just pick something funny."

"Fine, you pick," she huffs.

I flip through and find *Deadpool*, "Oh, I've been wanting to watch this one."

"I should've known you'd pick action."

Yeah, that damn movie was more uncomfortable than I thought it would be. The entire time they're banging like crazy in the movie, my mind kept drifting back to Raven in that damn bikini and rock hard nipples. What would've happened if I'd slipped those triangles to the side and looked at those perky tits? I'm in a freaking pair of basketball shorts, I can't hide much. I made several trips to the damn kitchen and bathroom. If she figures out I'm getting hard over here, she is going to bust my balls. Quite possibly literally.

CHAPTER 7

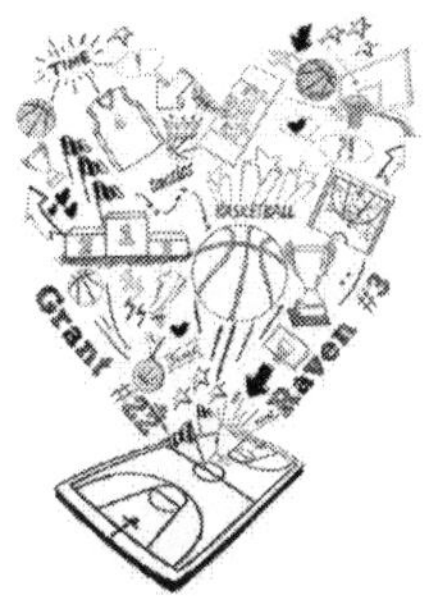

Raven-

Watching sex scenes with Grant was so damn weird. On the plus side, I caught a glimpse of Ryan Reynolds naked. The comments he made about me in my swimsuit were odd to say the least. He's never paid attention to what I was wearing before. Hell, just a few months ago he didn't even notice that I had boobs.

The movie has been off for a few minutes and we're just sitting here, both of us scrolling on our phones. Or well, I'm acting like my phone is the most interesting thing ever.

He clears his throat. "So see, it wasn't a total action movie."

"Yeah, it was kinda funny. I got to see Ryan Reynolds' ass, so not a total loss."

He laughs. "Really, his ass, that's what sticks out to you?"

I toss a pillow at him. "Shut up. I'm allowed to notice a guy's ass." I laugh, "Especially one that nice."

"I'm hurt you've never noticed my ass." He stands up and turns so that his backside is toward me. Pulling his shorts tight, he shakes his ass in my direction. "See, a nice ass." He starts moving like he's auditioning for *Magic Mike*.

About that time, his dad Greg comes in. “Son, are you having a damn seizure or something?” he says with a dumbfounded look on his face.

I bust out laughing and almost fall off the couch. Grant stops and looks at his dad, “Just showing off my assets.”

His dad snorts. “Well, don’t do it again. I thought we needed to call 911 and shove a stick in your mouth to keep you from biting your tongue.”

I laugh even harder and now his dad is, too. He’s getting mad. “Shut up, both of you. She was all lovesick over Ryan Reynolds’ bare ass on the movie.”

His dad, still laughing, tries to catch his breath. “Look, I just came to tell you guys that the food is ready.”

Grant stomps toward the kitchen. “Thank God, I’m starving!”

His dad follows him. “You sure we don’t need to check your sugar or something? I’m still not convinced what I saw in there wasn’t some kind of medical emergency.” As we enter the kitchen, his dad keeps ragging him. “Anne, we need to stop by CVS on the way home and get one of those at home drug tests. I think your son is on drugs.”

Everyone laughs, but Anne looks at him. “So he’s my son when you think he’s on drugs?”

Grant walks behind his mom, towering over her as he wraps his arms around her neck. “He’s just jealous that I have better moves than him. I was shaking my derriere for Rave as a comparison to Ryan Reynolds. Dad came in and I think I wounded his pride. I would say I have moves like Jagger, but mine are better.”

That receives snorts and laughs to which Anne shoves him off her and Grant moves to me, leaning on my shoulder. “Come on, Rave, tell them that I have the buttocks of a god. Don’t be shy. It could be compared to some Greek statues.”

I shove him off of me. “I’m like Greg. I thought he was having some sort of reaction.”

We keep laughing at his expense while we eat dinner. When he goes to leave, he stops. "Let me know what all you hear tomorrow. I'm sure there is going to be a bunch of bullshit. People are going to choose sides and unfortunately, I'm afraid it won't be Jo's. I don't want you busting someone in the mouth if they smart off about her." He looks over my shoulder to see if anyone is there. "Coach O doesn't play, he'll kick your ass off the team."

"I get it. But you're the one who goes around punching people, not me."

He shoves me in the shoulder as he walks out the door and I feel a little emptier, which I don't understand.

Finally, a month after the party that is still a topic of conversation amongst the school, hell, even the town, basketball season starts. Thank God because boredom is taking over my life. Don't get me wrong, practice takes up a lot of time, but since I'm not dating anyone, it can get a little lonely. Shane tried to call me several times the week following our break up, but once I didn't get more minutes on the extra phone, that stopped. In some ways it made me happy, but then again it hurt, too.

One thing that's different here versus my old school is that we have to dress up on game day. I feel weird walking into a gym dressed in my wrap dress and heels. I would just wear a pants suit like some of the other girls, but it's not always easy to find dress pants long enough for my legs. Sometimes jeans are a challenge, too, but most of the time I can get talls in them, dress pants aren't as easy. Both boys' Varsity and girls' Varsity are playing a little town an hour away. This school is so small they don't have a J.V. team so they scheduled our games back to back. The school, wanting to save money, made us ride one bus. Girls are definitely quieter on a trip than boys are. It's like they need to get pumped before a game where as I like my quiet time to focus and concentrate.

Our game is first so the guys sit behind the cheerleaders to watch us play. "All right, Quinn, let's do this!" I recognize Grant's voice from the stands.

The coach calls us in for our huddle. "What time is it?" he yells.

"GAME TIME!" We all respond.

"What time is it?"

"GAME TIME! GAME TIME! GAME TIME!"

A few minutes later, our center, Missy, is in the middle of the court for tip off. Our side of the gym erupts with the cheer. *"Boom, jump ball, get it get it, boom, jump ball, get it get it."* Missy knocks the ball in our direction. Crystal gets the ball and heads down the court, getting hemmed up she passes the ball to me, I go for the three and it goes in. We're on the board and our side jumps to their feet. "Way to start the game, Quinn!"

The score has pretty much been tied up for most of the game. We're now in the fourth quarter. The girl I'm constantly going up against is the same height as me, but she's a bigger girl. So when we both go up for the ball and her elbow comes down into my nose, it hurts like hell. The site of all the blood on the floor is an indicator of just how bad it is. Coach O rushes over to me with towels.

To her credit, the girl who hit me apologizes and so does her coach. "It's okay. It happens. We were both going after it."

"Come on, Quinn, let's get the medic to check out your nose." Coach O walks me toward the locker room while the assistant coach takes over. They have to wait for them to clean my blood off the floor before the game can resume. He beats on our locker room door and sticks his head in. Our guys are already in there dressing out for their game. "I need the medic out here to look at Quinn's nose."

As soon as he says that, the hall becomes crowded by our entire boys' team and the medic. After they gawk, the coach barks for them to get back in the locker room.

Grant stands there after everyone goes back in. Our medic pulls me into a small office, tipping my nose up. "Yeah, it looks like it just got hit really good. You're probably going to have a couple of black eyes. I don't think it's broken, though. I'm gonna pack it and you need to ice it. I'll get you some Tylenol then rest in here until it's time to leave."

The medic turns and leaves Grant in the office with me. "That's gonna hurt like hell later." He steps closer. "You should probably wake Warren and Tara when you get home. Show it to them and plan to stay home tomorrow. Tell them I'll get your work and bring it to you. It's Friday so you'll have the weekend to work on it."

I lay back on the small couch in the office. "Yeah, I'll do that."

"Hudson, it's warm up time!" Coach Leff calls Grant.

Grant throws his hand up to me, "See you in a little bit."

A few minutes later, I hear the girls filing into the locker room. Crystal comes in to check on me. "Hey, girl, you wanna shower? Coach said you could just to keep the packing in your nose so you don't get water up it for now."

"Yeah. What was the final score?"

She grins. "Sixty-eight to sixty-five, which we pulled out at the last minute. Missed you out there those last few minutes."

I follow her into the locker room and shower carefully before dressing in my warm-up suit and resting until the guys' game is over. They win by a little bigger spread, but still not huge. "Load up on the bus!" Coach O calls out to us.

I find a seat in the middle, hoping to stretch out and rest on the way home. Before I can lay my legs across the seat, Grant falls in next to me. "Why are you sitting here? There are going to be plenty of seats. I want to sleep on the way home."

He shrugs. "I know. I sat down so you can sleep on my shoulder. You need to keep your head elevated and if you rest it on the window, you're going to have an even worse headache."

He's right. "Fine." I settle in next to him. "But I don't want to talk. I want to sleep."

He shrugs and puts his earbuds in, letting me doze off. I wake to him lifting me up.

I barely wake up. "What are you doing?"

"I got you. I'm taking you home. Your head probably still feels like someone is standing on it."

I just nod and rest my head on his shoulder. "I'll take care of getting your car home."

I vaguely feel the ride home and then I'm being lifted out of the car. "Rave, can you stand up and open the front door?"

I stand up and fish my keys out of my pocket. When I open the door, he walks in behind me. I see the light on in the kitchen meaning one or both of my parents are waiting to see how the game went. They would've been there but they both had somewhere they had to be.

My face must look bad because my mom screams when I walk in the kitchen. I let Grant explain while I walk over to the fridge and grab another ice pack from the freezer, placing it on my face.

CHAPTER 8

Grant-

"What in the hell happened?" Warren asks after Tara screams. I knew they were going to have a fit. Rave's nose looks bad; it's gotten worse on the ride home. It's swelling pretty big, too. I'm glad to see that she's putting fresh ice on it.

"She caught an elbow. Her and the other girl went up for the ball and when they came down, the other girl's elbow caught her in the nose. It bled like crazy. Our medic looked at it. Says he doesn't think it's broken," I explain as I set her gym bag in the mud room where it goes. "I told her to stay home tomorrow, I'll get her work and stuff. She's gonna feel like crap."

Rave sits down at the bar, laying the ice pack across her nose. "It feels worse now than at the game."

I nod and pat her shoulder, "It looks a little worse, too."

She looks up at me and rolls her eyes. "Gee thanks, jerk."

Her dad laughs. "Yeah, Rave, I'm gonna say stay home."

"I think we need to take her to the doctor in the morning just to have it double checked," Tara says, taking a peek under the icepack on Rave's face.

"Mom, I'm fine."

Warren tries to calm Tara down. "Hun, she's just got a busted nose. If the medic doesn't think it's broken, then we should just let it heal."

She turns and glares at him with her hand on her hip. He quickly backpedals. "But if you'd feel better getting it checked then by all means, one of us will get her an appointment."

She nods and pulls Raven up off the stool. "Come on, honey, let's get you some medicine and get you in bed." She smiles at me. "Thank you, Grant, for bringing her home and taking care of her school work."

When I turn back to Warren, he grabs a couple of bottles of water out of the fridge. "Here, you probably need some hydration. I'm assuming her car is at the school?"

"Yeah, I figured she and I could go get it over the weekend if we need to."

He grabs his bottle of water. "If you've got time, we can just go get it now. I have a feeling her mom will keep her at home as much as possible." He takes a sip. "I'll call your parents and let them know what you're doing."

I nod. "Sure. It's no big deal. I'll go look in her gym bag, I think her keys are in there."

He brushes it off. "Nah, I got a set." He pulls them out of his pocket.

After we climb in my truck, I look over to him, "If Tara is determined to take her to the doc, Liberty Orthopedic sees all of the athletes at our school. I'm not sure who they used at her old school."

He laughs. "Yeah, I'm sure she's going somewhere tomorrow but thanks for that information. You'll figure out one day son, after you get married, that what you think is best or even know is best will never matter when Momma is worried about her baby. So I knew I just had to go with what she said."

I nod with a small chuckle. "It's okay, man. I've seen Dad do the same thing."

"We've learned after a lot of years it's best to agree or like sleeping on the couch," he says with humor as he slumps back into the seat of the truck.

The next day at school, on the way to jock gym class as everyone calls it, Collin stops me. "Hey, man, where is Raven? Joelle was looking for her, said she wasn't in the classes they share."

He looks frazzled so I touch his shoulder. "Well, she's at home. Her nose got busted pretty bad at the game last night. She caught an elbow."

He nods. "Oh. Joelle just really wanted to hang out with her I guess. We've got that trial coming up, and she'd come over to hang out at my house but hormones are flying. My mom has entered what they're calling her second trimester and she's trying to be super nurturing. So Joelle is like a baby deer. My mom is trying to coddle her to death. Plus, her mom is trying to make up for all the times Jo got pushed aside by everyone in the family." He sighs.

"Dude. That's doesn't sound like it's leaving you guys much time to—well, work out Jo's frustrations another way."

He half growls, half groans, "You have no idea."

"Dude," I say, rearing my head back. "Try a dry spell of about six months." Damn, it has been six months. I groan to accompany his groan.

I think for a second. "Here." I reach into my bag, grabbing the folder I was sticking Rave's stuff in. "I got most of her assignments for the day. I was going to run them over to her, but give them to Jo, sounds like she needs some vent time and I'm sure Rave would welcome the distraction from her mom doting on her." I grab my phone. "I'll text her to let her know the change of plans."

He smiles. "Thanks, man."

"So is everyone at your house adjusting to the fact that your mom is pregnant?" Right before the last party at the Daffin's farm, the mayor's wife (aka Collin's mom) found out she was pregnant, shocking them and everyone in the town.

Collin is sixteen and his brother fourteen, so yeah, needless to say all were shocked.

He nods. "Yeah, Dad is happier than I've ever seen him I think. Mom is an emotional roller coaster. She was crying over a commercial the other night about diapers. Then she squeals like some school girl. Brock is dealing, you know he'll be almost a sophomore when it gets here. He's been the baby for fourteen years, plus he's still a little grossed out by the fact that my mom had to have sex to get pregnant."

I bust out laughing. "He's that shook up by it, huh? I mean, I know he's had to have heard them."

He looks at me, shocked, and starts waving his arms around. "Is this like a normal thing? I mean Joelle said the same thing."

"NO! Our parents' bedroom is downstairs and we've never made it a habit of creeping outside their door."

I laugh even harder. "Sorry, dude. Didn't mean to scar you."

He shakes his head. "Man, I'd just gotten past that vision myself." He turns away, "I'll get this stuff to Jo."

I keep laughing as he walks off. I get a text back from Raven that's its cool about Jo bringing her work by. She'll see me when they come over to my house on Saturday.

Saturday rolls around and I hear the Quinn family come in. I go into the living room where they are. Raven's nose is bandaged up. "So what did the doc say?" I ask.

"There's a small hairline fracture, but not a lot they can do for it. I'd tried to tell mom that," she makes a frustrated face at her mom, "but she wouldn't listen."

Tara looks at her. "One day you'll have children and you'll understand."

I laugh and motion to the den. "Come on, let's go watch a movie or something."

"Nope," my dad says. "Warren and I are in there watching the football game."

I look at him like he's crazy. "What team are you watching? Alabama's not playing."

"No, but it's the ACC championship. We're following because of our fantasy football teams."

Raven laughs and I bark out a large laugh. "Really? Fantasy football? Dad, Warren, come on. Are you doing this with friends or online? If it's online, please don't take money from the guy who really needs to move out of his mom's basement."

Our moms and Raven start laughing. "Rave, I guess we'll watch the movie in here."

"Nope," my mom says. "We're watching a *Desperate Housewives* marathon on Lifetime. Just go watch it in your room."

I look at her like she's nuts because there's this big rule about no chicks in my room. Then again, they see it as Raven, but they don't know the thoughts that have been running through my head since I saw her at the party. But then Raven doesn't reciprocate those thoughts so it'll never matter.

"Ugh. Fine, come on, let's grab some snacks." I motion to our parents. "You know one of these days we're going to make our own plans on the weekend and not hang out with you guys."

Raven laughs as our moms make their way back from getting their wine out of the fridge. She follows me into the kitchen, we grab some cokes, chips and cookies before walking to my room.

After we put everything on my desk, I turn to her. "So, what movie are you in the mood for?"

She shrugs. "I really don't care. I'm kinda tired. I took some of the pain medicine they gave me at the doctor's office. I'm sure I'll just end up dozing off. Thanks for gathering up all of my homework, by the way. With practice and all, I hate to get behind."

"No problem. Come here, let me see it," I say, motioning to her nose. She stands in front of me with two black eyes and a big bandage. "You look pretty rough, Quinn."

She laughs and accidentally snorts. “Oh. That hurt.”

I place my thumbs on each side of her face, pulling back a little. I feel this pull to lean in and kiss her. My best friend. I can’t do that, though. “Actually, it doesn’t look as bad as I thought it would. It could’ve really been bad. I don’t think I’ve ever seen that much blood on the court.”

She sits back on my bed against the headboard. “Yeah, the worst part is they don’t want me to play for a week.”

“Damn. Even practice?” I ask, knowing what kind of torture it is to be told you *can’t* play. “That sucks.” I sit on the bed beside her.

“Yep and Coach O was totally on board with it. Although, if I got bumped in the nose, they’d probably revoke my badass card because I’d cry for sure.”

I laugh at her, “All right, so let’s pick a movie.” I flip on the TV and start scrolling through movies on Netflix. She gets really quiet and I notice she’s dozed off.

She looks so peaceful, I brush her hair back out of her face and it hits me that she’s not just hot, she’s beautiful. Then a noise comes from her mouth and she’s snoring. Holy crap—she sounds like a trucker.

I chuckle to myself as I settle in to watch the *Lethal Weapon* collection.

CHAPTER 9

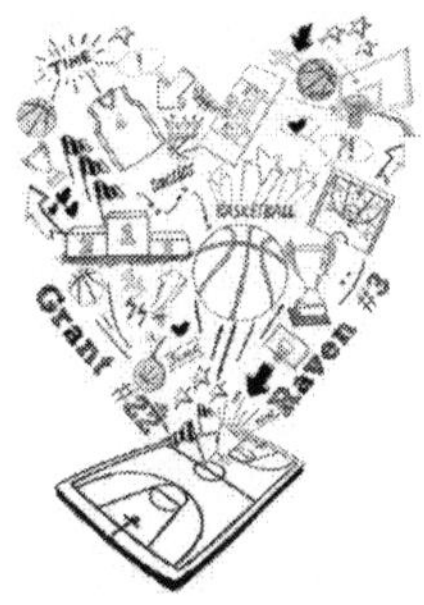

Raven-

I wake up to the sounds of explosions and sirens. It sounds like I'm in the middle of a shootout. I look up and realize we're watching one of the *Lethal Weapon* movies. "Really? You watch this all the time. I'd swear you have a crush on crazy Mel Gibson."

"Hey, it's a classic."

I shake my head. "I know. I know. But why does it have to be so damn loud?"

He starts laughing. "Well, because you snore like a trucker."

I shove him in the shoulder. "No, I do not."

"Oh yes, you do." He snorts, then he proceeds to pull out his phone and play it. "See."

And I really was snoring. Holy shit. "Shut up. My nose is swollen, so yeah, I'm gonna snore. Asshole, you better delete that."

"Maybe I should keep it; you know, just in case I ever need blackmail," he says with a smirk.

I sit up and wipe the sleep from my eyes. “You really are an ass.” I look over and see I’ve been sleeping for almost two hours. “Holy crap, I didn’t realize I was asleep that long.”

“Yeah, I’m already into the second movie,” he says, laying back with his fingers laced behind his head. His shirt rises up and I see a little strip of skin just above where his underwear and waistband sit. That sexy V is ever present. He’s still a little tan from the summer and a dark trail of hair sits there. Fuck, I’m staring, why in the hell am I staring? It’s not like I can have him. I’m just being creepy.

I shake my head and rub my eyes like I’m still really sleepy. “Well, I really am sorry. I didn’t mean to be a shitty guest.”

He sits up, wrapping one arm around my shoulders, like we always have. “Hey, you feel like crap, I get it. I’m not mad. Don’t be sorry.” He motions between us. “That’s how we can be us. Do you think I could sit here with some other random girl while she slept? No way. We can be cool like this.”

Yep, always in the friend zone. Any other girl he’d have been trying to get into her panties.

“Thanks.”

He shifts back over to his side of the bed. “So, did you and Jo have a good time yesterday?”

I roll my shoulders, thinking about Jo and all she’s going through. “Yeah, she’s just getting stressed out with the trial coming up. Then, she thinks James and Clem are seeing each other and won’t tell her.”

He looks confused. “Why wouldn’t they tell her about it? And wait, I thought Clem and Harrison had a thing going on?”

I shake my head. “I guess Clem and Harrison are like us, just friends. I don’t know why they wouldn’t tell her. She is more upset that they are keeping it from her than if they are dating.”

“I get that. It’s more about the betrayal feeling,” he says with understanding.

"So she just needed to vent. It was good to get a little break from my mom trying to coddle me."

He laughs. "I figured you'd feel that way. And I could tell from the way Collin acted that she needed you. So that's why I sent your stuff with her."

I think about what all he did for me the other night. He was a really good friend. I reach over and touch his arm. "Thanks for taking care of me the other night after the game. It kind of occurred to me that you're an awesome friend even when I've been being a bitch sometimes."

He shrugs, turning back to the movie. "Hey, you had your reasons and that's what friends do. Real friends, anyway."

I lean back against the headboard beside him to watch the movie, which I can tell he's ready to get back to so I stop talking.

~*~

Tonight was our first home game. It was an awesome win and I got to be a big part of it. Grant and his family were there cheering me on. I guess it is awesome that we play for the same school now. My dad was there supporting me like always, it sucks my mom had to miss it for work, or she would've been there yelling louder than anyone in the stands.

I'm finishing my sandwich in the kitchen with Dad when his phone rings. He answers it, dropping his sandwich to the counter top. "Yes, I'm on my way."

He grabs his keys. "Come on. Your mom was in an accident. She's at the hospital, they said she's in surgery."

I grab my shoes and run out the door behind him, putting them on in his truck on the way. I make a quick phone call to Grant's dad Greg to let him know what's going on.

We arrive at the hospital in Monroe in record time. We're rushed through the emergency room to a surgical waiting room. Soon, Grant and his family are sitting with us.

There are moments in your life that you just know you'll never forget. This is one. I'll never forget the look on the surgeon's face when he walked into the waiting room. It's a distant look of defeat, but I can also see the sadness behind it. He steps in front of my dad. I've already tunneled out. Bits and pieces of what he's saying make it through to my brain. *Extensive internal damage. -We did all we could do. -Every measure has been taken. -I'm sorry for your loss.*

Suddenly, a loud sobbing breaks through the roaring going through my head. I look over to see my dad collapsed in a chair, shaking.

I look in front of me to see Grant and Anne standing there. I feel my stomach lurch as I run to the trash can and heave into it. Once I have nothing left in my stomach, I back away from it and feel lightheaded. I can't control my body as it starts to wilt to the ground. Before I get there, a strong set of arms lift me up and start to carry me over to a chair. Once he sits down, his arms wrap around me and he strokes my hair.

Hours later, I'm lying in bed all cried out staring at the ceiling. Grant is lying beside me as I'm tucked into his side. The warmth of his body soothes me. It all hits me so hard. My mom was here earlier today, now she's gone. How do I live without my mom? Even through all the shit with Shane, she was there for me, even if I was a total bitch to her. All those times I yelled at her that she didn't understand. The nights I heard her crying after we would have a fight about him. I did so many shitty things I regret.

Then she'd do cool things like going to get our nails done. Watching her and her best friend made me hope that one day I'd have a friend like that. The closest I have is lying here beside me and something tells me that Grant will never be the type to go get drunk while getting our nails done.

Moments flash through my mind like a movie. Helping me blow out my candles. Taking me to get my first bra. Her shoving cake in my dad's face or cracking an egg on his head when they'd argue in the kitchen. Finally, exhaustion takes over and I pass out.

CHAPTER 10

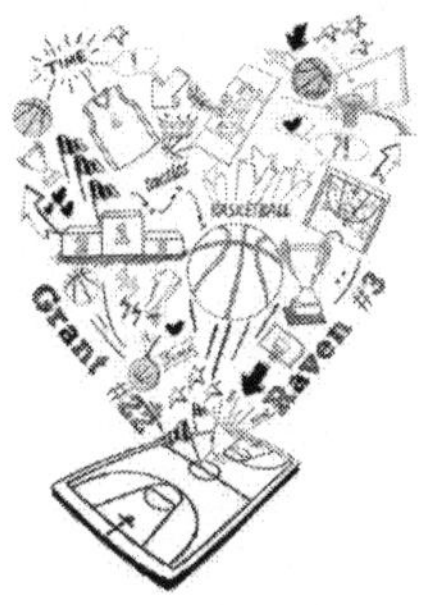

Grant-

One minute, we are on this Earth and the next minute, we aren't. That's the lesson I'm trying to take from this. Tara was here, she was a sweet lady, my mom's best friend and my best friend's mom. Now, she's just gone. No more pinching my cheek when it's full of cake in her kitchen. Never again will I hear her voice from the stands cheering me on or calling me Granny Grant when I walk through her front door. *Why she called me granny instead of grampy, or why period, I'll never know.*

Warren is just going through the motions. My dad has tried being his shoulder, because that's what friends do, but he won't take the shoulder. He just keeps pushing forward. He wants to go back to work this week. Tara has only been gone a week and a half. Raven is supposed to be going back to school tomorrow, but it worries me because she's pretty much been locked up in her room. It all seems rushed to me, but I'm not them, and as much as I'm trying to understand, it's something my mom says I won't be able to. That everyone has to grieve in their own way.

Coach O and the basketball teams, both girls' and boys', have been bringing dinners by. Not that either of them have really eaten anything during this time.

Even though they live in between Greenville and Everly, not in the city limits, Collin's parents, the mayor, Thad, and his wife, Ella Mae, came by to check on them.

Joelle and Collin both said that Ella Mae knew Tara and my mom from college. They were all in the same sorority and that she's been heartbroken over all of this. I'm sure her pregnancy hormones aren't helping, or that's what I've been told.

Crystal approaches me after class. "So, Raven texted me and says she's coming back tomorrow."

I shift my bag. "That's what she says. I don't know about basketball, though."

"Coach says it's all up to her. Whenever she's ready to come back, the spot is hers," she says softly, looking at the ground.

"Yeah, that's great," I say before walking away.

I can't help but think about lying in her bed that night holding her so close. She cried until she fell asleep and then she kept mumbling things I couldn't make out. I only know that's the most complete I've ever felt in my life and I feel like shit about it because to be in that moment came at a cost.

Then the asshole of the year, Shane, had the fucking nerve to come by her mother's viewing. Stood right up in the front of the church and shook her father's hand, saying he was sorry for their loss. They had Warren on so much medication, I don't think he really thought about who it was. My dad left a damn bruise on my arm from holding me back. I watched as he hugged Raven for a little too long. Whispered things in her ear. I waited and followed him out the door. That smug fucking look on his face when he turned to me. *"If it isn't the golden boy basketball star."*

Pointing my finger at him, I state firmly, "You stay the fuck away from her. She doesn't need your bullshit right now."

He shakes his head. "Oh, I think I'm just what she needs. She'll need me to cry on. She'll always want me." He steps closer to me. "And do you know why? Because I make her feel beautiful. I make her think she's just as pretty as all the other girls I fuck that she doesn't know about."

"That's where you're wrong. She is the most beautiful girl in the world. As far as those other girls you were fucking while you had her, that was stupidity on your part. Because you lost her. What kind of sick bastard are you to prey on someone who just lost their mother? What's your fucking problem? Mommy and Daddy didn't hug you enough?"

He laughs. "Fuck you and my parents. Her mom hated me so what does it matter to me? Oh, I didn't lose her. I can get her tomboy ass back anytime I want to and if you really believed she was the most beautiful girl in the world, you'd have been fucking her a long time before I was. Rather than playing basketball with her like she's just one of the damn guys, which I can see the mistake there." My body is trembling with pure damn anger, but the officer directing the traffic at the edge of the parking lot is keeping me from hitting him. He's right about one thing. Why haven't I noticed her until now? He turns to get in his truck, "But I will say you aren't missing much. She just lays there like a fuck doll. But...I got my dick wet, that's what matters."

I step toward him, cop be damned I'm gonna beat his ass. A hand grabs me and then Collin's deep voice says, "Get the fuck outta here, buddy, or Chief Reed will escort you away."

The douche smirks at us, getting into his truck. I start back toward him again, but Collin tugs me back. He manages to get in front of me and starts pushing me to the entrance of the funeral home.

Once he drives out of the parking lot, Collin turns to me. "While I really wanted you to kick his ass because I heard everything he said, Rave really doesn't need you in trouble or causing a big scene."

My heart is pounding in my ears. I wanna beat his ass so bad. Knowing Collin is right, though, I nod. "Yeah, I know. Thanks for stopping me." I look around to see we really didn't draw a crowd. "Don't say anything to her about this. Maybe he'll just crawl back into whatever hole he came out of."

A part of me wonders if he's tried to get up with her since that night. She hasn't said anything to me, but then again she probably wouldn't. All of the shit he was spewing about her echoes through my head. As much of a dick as it makes me sound, I'm angry that he felt the need to fill me in on their sex life. I hate that she had a sex life with him. I hate that she's had a sex life with *anyone*. How can I judge her, though, for having sex? Jeez. Where is all of this coming from? Am I feeling all of this because Tara's gone? I can't really say that because I started getting confused before that. Damn, when did my life get so confusing.

Three months later, we've been through Thanksgiving, Christmas and started a new year without her mom. She moves through the halls, going to class and practice. She manages to do all of these things without even appearing to be awake. She's lost part of her spark on the court and she never talks. Everyone is coming to me about it, like I can do something. I don't know what the fuck Warren is doing but it's like he's just checked out. I mean it's only been that long, but still, he's got to be a parent. She's already lost one and it's almost like she's lost two. "Dad, have you talked to Warren?"

He rests his hip on the counter in our kitchen. "Yeah, he went back to work so I've seen him a couple of times. Why?"

"I think Rave is drowning. She's just going through the motions at school, basketball, basically life. I'm worried." I try to express just how worried I truly am. I feel like my best friend is suffering and slipping away. Basketball has always been her life and now it's like she's just showing up.

My dad just takes it in, nodding. "Okay, I'll talk to him and have your mom look in on Raven. She may just need a woman. You know?"

I nod. "Thanks, Dad."

On the way back to my room, my phone chimes. I look down at it. It's Tabitha. What is she doing texting me? She got a great opportunity to do a year abroad. That was one of the reasons we broke up, but it was also just time. I didn't see it then, but I do now. At first I made dumb mistakes like Ciara, then I tried dating with Cher, but that didn't work. So now I've been single with the casual make out session. I open up the message icon to read her text.

Tabitha: I know you haven't heard from me in forever. I don't always have service and my text rates are freakin' nuts. But, I just heard about Raven's mom, please tell her how sorry I am.

Me: Thanks. I'll let her know.

Keep it short and sweet, no use making things confusing. Then there is another ping.

Tabitha: How are you and your parents? I know how close all of you are.

Me: We're getting there. It's been hard on my mom especially. I'm worried about Raven.

Tabitha: I can only imagine. I don't know what I would do. On another note I heard in a Facebook message from Cher that Rave was dating a pretty rough guy a while back. Has she stayed away from him?

I'm going to seem like a damn chump, but her bringing up that ass makes me think.

Me: Yeah, she has. Can I ask you a question? I mean it may be really shitty of me to ask. Just warning.

Tabitha: Shoot. We're still friends.

Me: Were you ever jealous of Raven and the relationship I have with her?

Tabitha: LOL oh so her boyfriend didn't like it?

Me: No he didn't.

Tabitha: Well it's not shocking. I mean once you pull your head out of your ass and realize she's a girl you're going to fall in love. To be honest that's one of the reasons I knew it was time for us to be over. I knew I was really on temporary, but Rave, she'd always be there. So let me guess these questions are because you've

started to pull that head out and you're confused.

Me: Maybe. I mean her last boyfriend hurt her. Physically, emotionally and mentally. I think maybe I'm just trying to save her and then I think about seeing her in a bikini and I'm confused again.

Tabitha: LMAO. It's happening. I knew it would.

Me: This is fucking weird. I'm sorry. I shouldn't bother you with this.

Tabitha: No, it's not. When we broke up we both said that we wanted to stay friends and I know unlike others we meant it. I haven't stayed in touch like we planned, but I meant it. Trust me looking from the outside in, you're falling for her. You just never paid attention until now. Crap I gotta go, I have a lecture to get to. Go after her. Hit me up on Facebook sometime. That doesn't cost as much.

Me: Thanks Tabby you really are a great friend. Some guy is going to be lucky to have you.

Tabitha: Thanks.

Well, fuck...

What do I do with those answers?

CHAPTER 11

Raven-

Walking through the front door of my house is strange. I glance into the empty living room where no pumpkins were sat out this year for fall decorations and no tree was put up for Christmas. For my entire life I've been used to walking in after practice and smelling my mom's cooking or hearing my parents in the kitchen with the take-out they picked up. Now, I hear nothing.

Moving into the kitchen, I know Dad is home because there are empty beer bottles on the counter after I'd cleaned it off this morning. I look out in the backyard and he's sitting in a patio chair, just staring out into space.

I slide open the door. "Hey, Dad, what do you want for supper?"

He jumps at the sound of my voice. "Oh. Sorry, I didn't hear you come home. I'm not really hungry, sweetie. I had a late lunch. Why don't you just run and grab something for yourself?" He fishes some money out of his pocket. "Here you go."

I take the money. "Okay, but I'm bringing you back something, too. You might get hungry later." Because I'm pretty sure he didn't eat that lunch he claims he did. I should heat one of the bazillion casseroles in the freezer, but staying in this house is driving me crazy. It's way too quiet and lonely, but at the same time I want to be left alone. I find myself sitting in the park most afternoons watching kids play. But today, I'm just going to go back and battle the echoing silence.

Once I pull into the Sub Hut parking lot, I see kids from school and I sigh. I really don't want to see people right now. Every time they give me this look. The look that says I'm sorry you lost your mom, I'm glad it wasn't mine, but this is awkward so I'll just hug you and tell you how sorry I am. I, in turn, feel like throwing up and just want to hide.

I park at the end and try to slip in the door without everyone seeing me. Once I'm in line, I feel someone behind me in line, closer than I'm comfortable with. I turn to say something rude when I see it's Shane.

"Can you give me some space?" I motion for him to step back.

He looks at me with a softness. "Sorry." He takes a small step back. "Hey, I just wanted to say I know things didn't end great with us, but if you need anything just let me know. Even if it's just to yell and scream. Just call me."

He's trying to be nice I guess. "Um, thanks. I'm just ordering my dad and I some food, then going back home. Neither of us are much for cooking right now." He didn't ask you what you were doing, dumb ass. Way to be a head case, Raven.

He nods, shoving his hands in his pockets. "Yeah, I imagine." Thank God he's just going along with it. He motions for me to step forward as it's my turn to order. "Well, my offer stands."

"Thanks," I say with a small smile. After I order our subs, I run into Collin on the sidewalk.

"Hey," I say with a small wave.

"Hey, girl," he says, juggling a couple of bags.

I point to the bags. "What's all that?"

He sighs almost comically. "Well, my mom is craving pickles, Cap'n Crunch and coffee ice cream. Jo is craving some Reese's cups, cookie dough ice cream and chips."

I laugh, the first real laugh I've had in a few days. "Jo's craving?"

He looks uncomfortable. "Yeah, it's...ugh."

"Oh!" I laugh again. "So, your mom's pregnancy cravings and Jo's monthly cravings are lining up today."

"Yeah." He motions to the bag in my hand. "You grabbing supper?"

"Mmm hmm." I nod. "I didn't feel like cooking tonight." I don't add that neither my dad nor myself have used an appliance in our kitchen except the fridge since Mom died.

"Well, I better get this stuff back to the house before they call and add more to the list." He chuckles.

"Yep, you better. See you at school."

"See ya." He lifts an elbow to wave, walking away.

When I get back home, I see that Greg's truck is there. When I walk into the kitchen with the subs, I see I've interrupted something. "Hey, Dad, I got you an Italian on wheat."

His face softens. "Thanks, sweetie. Ah, Grant is out back shooting some hoops. Why don't you go practice with him?"

"Is everything okay?" I ask with concern.

He gives me a slight nod. "Yeah, sweetie. Just go out there. Greg and I are talking privately."

I nod and go outside. Hearing the ball bouncing against the concrete, I find Grant *shirtless* and sweaty. My belly just did some kind of flip flop.

"Hey."

He looks up and passes me the ball. "Hey. Where were you?" He swipes some sweat from his face.

"I went to grab a couple of subs for Dad and me for supper. Ran into Collin buying a crap load of craving food." Why am I rambling?

"Oh, I'm guessing he went for his mom. He told me he had to run to the Frosty King at eleven the other night for her," he says, amused.

"Well, for her and Jo," I reply without thinking.

His head arcs up with a crazy look. "Jo? You don't? She's not?"

I realize what he's thinking. "Oh God! No! She's got a different case of hormones going on." Crap, I just told Grant that Jo is on her period. I put the ball to my forehead. "Shit, don't repeat that. I'm sure Jo doesn't want you knowing her business."

He laughs as I pass the ball back to him. "Don't worry, I'm not talking about her *girl* stuff. It was bad enough the first time I had to hear about it in living color."

"Ugh! Shut up. That was probably up there with the top three embarrassing moments of my life." It so was. Waking up the morning I got my very first period in bed with Grant was right up there with going to school naked. Anne having to call my mom after I ran out of the room screaming. Grant looking like he may pass out or throw up was horrible and then he was nervous to talk to me for days after.

He takes a shot and I grab the ball. "How do you think I felt? My dad tried to explain it to me first while mom was calling your mom, he got all red and flustered. My mom came in and tried to save the situation, but still I was pretty scarred." He shakes his head. "All I can say is that it scored me points as an *understanding* boyfriend."

I shoot the ball and it goes in. "Ugh. Leave it up to you to gain off of my misfortune."

He rolls his shoulders as he grabs the ball. "Hey, I had to live through it. I should get the badge for it."

"Ugh. Let's quit talking about this. What are you guys doing over here?"

He grabs the ball after he shoots it and motions for us to sit on the bench by the court. "Dad just wanted to check on Warren. He hadn't talked to him in a few days, he's been kind of distant."

"So what are you doing here?"

He throws a sweaty arm around my shoulder. "Do I really need an excuse to come see my favorite girl?"

I'm jolted by those words and I feel it from him he is, too. He's always called me his best friend, friend, sister from another mister or just his girl, like a bro. His favorite girl, just the way he said it made my skin tingle. He stands up quickly from the bench. "So are you ready for your last game this Friday?"

I shrug. Really my heart hasn't been in the game since my mom died. How the team still ended up in the Regional Playoffs is a pure miracle. "Yeah. I'm actually just ready for the season to be over this year and I feel really bad about that. I mean I have this great opportunity with this team and it's like I'm wasting it."

He steps directly in front of me, pulling me to my feet, tilting my head to look up at him. "You aren't wasting anything. You've been through some bad shit this year. Most people couldn't go out there and play like you have. I know you haven't been yourself on the court, but hell, you're still kicking ass out there."

My chest feels like it's heaving. Something about his eyes, the way he's looking at me. My nipples get hard and I want to kiss him. I want to kiss my best friend. He leans down a little closer and I know he's feeling this, too. We break apart when we hear the door to my house open and voices coming out.

We're both breathing heavy when our dads make it around the fence. "Hey, you two, who won?" Greg asks.

Grant shrugs. "We were just messing around, Dad. No keeping score. I think we're both a little tired of basketball and ready for our seasons to be over." I nod in agreement.

Greg motions to Grant, “Come on, let’s go. I’m sure Rave is ready to woof down her sub. It smelled great in there.”

They leave and I follow my dad into the house. For the first time since my mom died, we sit at our kitchen island and eat together. It’s in silence, but it happens. Maybe we’re healing. Just maybe.

CHAPTER 12

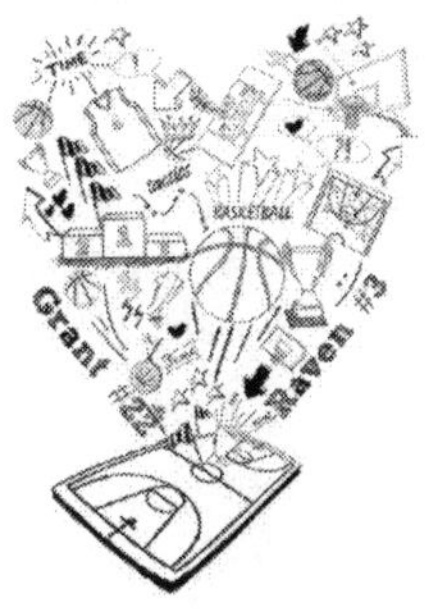

Grant-

I almost kissed her. I was frustrated that I didn't get to. "What are you so uptight about?" Dad asks on our way home.

"Huh?" Oh yeah, besides my pants being tight. "Just tired, not really uptight." I look more his direction. "How did it go with Warren?"

He shrugs and sighs. "Fine, I guess. I know he's still hurting, but I made an effort to ask a lot about Raven so maybe he'll think about her and what he's missing out on."

"Dad."

"Grant, the man is my best friend. He loves his daughter; he's just going through a heartache I hope I never have to. We talked, he seems like he's coming around. If I see that he's still slipping or Raven comes to me, I'll say more. But until then, I can't make the man do anything."

I stare out the window. "Okay."

My dad continues to make general conversation, about school and basketball, all while I stare at the fall-colored trees flying by. I almost kissed her, I wanted to kiss her, to feel her lips on mine, slipping my tongue in her mouth. Fuck, I gotta stop thinking about it. I don't need to embarrass myself in front of my dad.

It's Friday night and both teams are playing Greenville in Greenville for the Regional Finals. It's got to be weird for Raven playing her old teammates. They were matched up one time before this year, but it was while she was out after her mom died.

We've already won our game, now the girls' game is beginning. Since it's a Regional game, they gave us an intermission of sorts between games. Normally the games are back to back and I wouldn't have gotten to watch the start of this game. *"Boom. Jump ball, get it get it, jump ball, get it get it."* This is the first time in years our girls' team has been to Regionals.

"The ball is knocked to number three for the Everly Pirates' Raven Quinn. She makes her way down the court and up for the three, it goes in."

"All right, Quinn! Let's see some action," I yell from the stands. Raven actually seems more like herself playing tonight as I watch her smile, making some serious plays. I'm pretty sure it has to do with Warren being here tonight. The announcers have said her name all night. She's had a bunch of assists and several baskets.

They're down to the last quarter, our girls are up by three. It feels like the walls are pulsing in here. It's been a tight game all night. Shit, they just called a personal foul on Crystal. Greenville sets up to do free throws. Now they're tied up. I'm practically holding my breath. There's only thirteen seconds left in the game. Missy bullies the ball down the court and passes it to Raven, the entire gym is on their feet to see if we are going into overtime tonight. Raven shoots at the three-point line just as the buzzer sounds. The place goes quiet just before the ball swishes into the net. Within seconds the floor is covered with people cheering and hugging. Making my way through the crowd, I find Raven jumping around with her team. I snatch her into my chest and kiss her.

She pulls back, shocked. I put my hand on top of her head, messing up her ponytail. "Good game, Quinn."

She nods, breathing hard. "Thanks." Turning back to her teammates, I see her dad headed over. My dad throws his arm around my shoulders, as my mom hugs me and then runs to Rave.

"Good game, son."

"Thanks, Dad."

He turns toward me. "What was that kiss about?"

Shit, he's right, I just did that in front of a gym full of people. "Nothing, just congratulating her. Heat of the moment kind of thing. Hell, after our game I almost wanted to kiss Preston." Total lie.

My dad laughs, shaking his head. "Well, I'm glad to know you didn't do that. Rave is a lot prettier."

I see some of Rave's old team talking to her. A couple of the guys I know from here come over to congratulate me. "Hell of a couple of games, man. Still pissed you guys took Rave from us."

"Yeah, he breaks up with me and then takes one of our star players," Cher butts in.

I give her a brief hug. "Hey, girl, you guys played great, though. That was a tight game."

"Thanks. I do miss Rave being on the team, though."

"I'm sure. I taught her everything she knows," I joke. Cher shoves me in the shoulder just as I hear Coach O whistle, which means celebration time is over and it's time to load the bus. "Gotta go. Good to see you guys." They wave their goodbyes as I walk away.

As we start loading the bus, I realize I'm waiting on her. I want to share a seat with her like I did the night she was hurt.

I glance around the parking lot looking for her and see her talking to Shane. She's got a little distance between the two of them, but still she's talking to him.

I call out. "Rave, we gotta go!"

She looks at me and nods. Turning back to him, she says something and comes running to the bus.

“Hey, I was saving you a seat,” I say to her as we climb the stairs of the bus.

“Oh really? Let me guess, a seat with you?”

“I don’t know, you haven’t showered tonight. I might put you in the back of the bus,” I joke as I sit down, reaching out for her to pull her down with me.

She gets settled in the seat, scrunching down and putting her knees on the back of the seat in front of us. “So you had a great game tonight,” she states.

“Yeah. So did you. You were on freakin’ fire out there. It’s like you found your edge again.”

“I guess I felt like it was time to move on, quit looking for her in the stands.” Damn, I never thought about that, her mom really did try to be at as many games as she could. “I think Dad being there helped. He said the other night when you guys came over Greg asked a lot of questions about how I was doing. He realized he didn’t really know, so he had to come out of the funk he was in.” Good, so Dad’s talk did help.

“Good. I have to admit I was worried about both of you.” I mimic her in the seat, scrunching down. “So what did the douche want?”

She shrugs, looking at her hands in her lap. “Just to talk, tell me I played a good game. Tell me he’s there if I need someone to talk to.”

Bullshit. I fucking hate that guy. He’s trying to manipulate her again. “You don’t believe him, do you?”

“I think he’s just trying to be nice. Taking pity on me. Anyway, I was just being polite to him.”

I want to tell her all of the shit he was spouting in the parking lot of the funeral home, but I won’t. She doesn’t need that shit. It would just bring down the high she’s on right now.

She clears her throat. “So um...what was that about after the game?”

I know what she’s asking about. She’s asking about the kiss, but I’m going to make her say it. “What was what about?”

She rolls her eyes and looks at me like I'm an idiot. "You kissing me. Everyone saw it."

She seems embarrassed, maybe I've been misreading how this is going. I could've sworn the other day at her house the feeling was mutual. So I just shrug it off. "Just congrats, that's all. Caught up in the moment, I guess. Hell, I almost kissed Preston after our game. Tonight was exciting." I better not have to tell that lie to anyone else tonight.

She laughs. "Okay. It just...well, it caught me off guard. Crystal asked me if things had changed between us. I was like no. Not that I'm aware of."

I turn and stare out the window as she props her head on my shoulder. "Yeah, wouldn't want that," I mumble.

CHAPTER 13

Raven-

Of course he was just kissing me to congratulate me. Now I've been awake half the damn night remembering how his lips felt on mine.

My phone ringing brings me out of my thoughts. I see that it's Shane. I groan, staring at my ceiling. "Really, as if I need more shit to think on right now." I swipe the green arrow on my phone. "Hello."

"Hey, it's Shane."

"Yeah, I know. Hey."

"I was wondering if you wanted to get together and maybe grab some lunch?"

What can I say? What do I want to say? He's been nothing but nice, but he made an ass out of me. I need to give myself some time. "I can't today. I have to help my dad with some stuff." Total lie. "But, maybe another day."

"Okay, that works." I hear him sigh. "I just...I just wanted to say I'm sorry about everything that happened while we were dating. You were better to me than I deserved and I constantly fucked it all up."

What do I say to that? Is this really him talking? Is it pity? What is it? "Thanks. Just text me another day about lunch. I just—I really gotta go help my dad now."

"Okay, babe. Good talking to you."

I clear my throat. "You, too." *Babe.*

Once we hang up, I flop back on the bed. "Damn it. Why does this all have to be so complicated?"

My phone starts ringing again, but this time I know the ringtone. It's Joelle. "Hello."

"Oh my God! You are never going to believe this!"

"Okay, what am I not going to believe?" I ask, wondering what has Jo, of all people, so excited. Jo is seriously the type of person who would walk in a room, say something and then be like, "Oh, by the way, the building is on fire."

"Collin's parents have decided to take a group of us to Monarch, Colorado during Spring Break skiing. They say that the slopes are open until like April out there. Our break is in three weeks in the middle of March!"

"Wait. What? How? Huh? Slow down and start over."

"Okay." She lets out a huge breath. "Collin's parents normally take him and his brother on some exotic trip every year for Spring Break, but since Ella Mae is six months pregnant, they can't do that. As early as break is this year, unless we go to South Florida, it's too cold to go to the beach. So they decided to rent out a small ski lodge, one of those mom and pop places. They are chartering a bus and taking some of us to Monarch, Colorado, skiing." I swear I can feel her vibrating through the phone.

"So wait, am I invited? Is that what you're trying to say?"

"YES! Collin invited me, of course. Then you, Grant, Dallas, my sister and brother, Vivian, Clem and his brother is inviting a few of his friends from ninth grade."

Shaking my head, I'm still trying to make sense of all of this. "So how much do we have to pay? How can we do that? The basketball team won Regionals last night."

"That's the best part, they got this great deal on the bus and lodge so they're covering that. All we have to bring is our spending money and rental money for skis and stuff. The basketball part, even if you guys go to State, it'll be over by then."

I sit up in the bed, all of this finally making sense to me. "Are you freakin' serious right now?!" I look around my room. "We are getting a pretty much all expenses paid trip to Colorado?"

"YES! YES!" I can hear who I am assuming is Collin in the background telling her to calm down.

"Holy crap. I need to go talk to my parents." Then it hits me. *Deep breath.* "I mean my dad. I'm sure he'll be okay with it since Collin's parents are going." I shake my head. "Holy crap, I still can't believe this."

"Believe it, sister. Now go talk to your dad. I need to go kiss my boyfriend again for having awesome parents."

I laugh. "Okay. Tell Collin I love having him as a friend and tell his parents thank you."

We say our goodbyes and hang up. I practically trip in my sheet trying to get to my bedroom door. "Dad! Dad!"

He comes up out of his chair as I enter the living room. "Are you okay?'

I jump up and down in place. "Yes! Oh my God!" I start rattling about what Jo said and I can tell he's getting a little lost. "So my question is can I go, Daddy, please?"

He gives me a chuckle. That's the first time I've seen him even crack a smirk in months. "If I understood all of that correctly then yes." He sits back down in his chair. "So the Atwoods will be with you guys and I only have to send money with you for extra stuff?"

"Yes! Oh my God, Dad, isn't this awesome?" I can't stop smiling. My face is really starting to hurt.

"Yes, it's great and really nice that they decided to share a vacation like this. I have to say, if we lived in Everly I'd vote him in for mayor again. There is a lot to be said for a man who is willing to take a group of teens on a skiing trip. It says he's not a greedy man. He's willing to share and that is a man I can stand behind."

I throw my arms around my dad's neck. "Thank you, Daddy! Thank you!"

He hugs me back tight. "How about I run to the store and grab us a couple of steaks for tonight? I'll grill them. We need to do some catching up."

I pull back a little. "Sounds great. Do you mind if I go online and look at some ski outfits?"

"No, sweetie. You have that one card for emergencies, just use it if you find something while I'm not here. Don't go too crazy, though."

"Yes, sir!" I squeal, running back to my room.

I call Clem. She screams as soon as she answers. After a few minutes of discussing the trip, I hang up and start looking on the computer for outfits. I've never bought ski clothes and it's damn sure not something many people in Alabama have to worry about buying.

My phone rings again and it's Grant's ringtone. I guess he's gotten the phone call now. I swipe the screen "Hey, I guess Collin has called you?"

"Yeah, that's some crazy shit, huh? You're going, right?"

"Well, yeah. Dad said it was cool, I'm looking online at ski suits now. He ran to the store to grab him and me a steak to grill tonight."

"That's great. So are you going to stay on the bunny slopes with me? You know, since we've never skied before."

I laugh. "I'm sure there will be quite a few of us on the bunny slopes. Not many people from here have snow skied. Stick us on a pair of water skis, hell yeah. But not snow."

I hear him chuckle. "Very true." I can hear his mom in the back ground. "Mom says to look and see what they have for me. I'm not sure why I can't look for my own clothes, but anyway."

"Because she knows as hot natured as you are, you'll think you only need a wind suit and you'll come home with pneumonia or something."

I hear him snort. "Another true statement."

"Okay, well, I'll look and see what all I find. I'll probably call your mom if I do find anything."

"Sounds good. I really don't care about clothes."

I bark out a laugh. "You'll care if they're not warm enough and you're freezing your balls off."

"That's sweet of you, always looking out for my balls."

I shake my head. "Shut up, perv. I gotta go. I'll get up with you later."

"Cool."

Scrolling through, I find several items I want to buy, but I have to remember this will probably be the only time for years that I'll get to use them.

My chest suddenly feels warm and I just know that if my mom were here, she'd be so excited that I was getting to do something like this. I look over at the picture of us on my nightstand and smile, I know she's with me.

Having steaks with my dad is surprisingly easy. He's actually talking to me. Asking me questions. "So I have to ask," he says with a small smile. "Why did Grant kiss you last night on the court?"

My stomach flutters just thinking about it. I try not to get flushed over it. I pick at my potato on my plate. "He was just caught up in the moment after the games. Believe me, I asked because I got asked five seconds after it happened."

"Are you sure? It looked like more than that from where I was standing."

I put my fork down. "Come on, Dad, it's Grant. Neither of us think of each other like that. Plus, I mean come on, that was in no way what I would consider a romantic kiss. It was just sweaty lips pressed flat against each other."

He shakes his head and goes back to eating. “Okay, whatever you say.” After chewing a piece of steak, he clears his throat. “Rave, I want to say I’m sorry. I missed so many of your games this year. Hell, I really missed so much of you. Your mom would be disappointed in me and how I’ve handled things.”

I sigh and just nod. We both sit super quiet for a few minutes. I can’t handle the uncomfortable tension. I look at him with a grin. “She would’ve really kicked your butt for not getting a tree.”

He snorts, almost sending beer out of his nose. “Yes, she would have.” He stops, looking down. “I’ve been moving in my own fog. And until Greg stopped by the other day and asked me about some of your games and grades, I didn’t realize I’d frozen you out.”

I reach over the table and grab his hand. “Dad, it’s okay, I have been, too. I was walking around here silent; I could’ve talked to you. I mean I miss Mom. My heart still aches when I lay in my bed at night, but I had a dream about her the other night. She was walking on a beach and I ran to her, she hugged me really tight. I could feel it. She made some smart remark about how crappy I’d played the night before. *Which was true, by the way.* She told me to get my head out of the fog of grief and play damn ball. She said if I made her look like an idiot bragging about how good I was and then playing like crap, she’d haunt me for the rest of my life. So I decided to take her advice.” I stop, thinking about how absolutely nuts I sound. I pull my hand back and wave it around. “I mean I know it probably really wasn’t anything, but it made me think. I’m sure this sounds stupid. I don’t know, it made me feel something in my chest.”

My dad smiles. “Don’t discount it, it’s not stupid. We all know your mom liked to get the last word. What better way than in a dream? Either way, it was the push you needed so take it as that. You rocked that court last night. Plus, I mean we both knew your mom, she was the kind of person who’d haunt someone.” We both laugh about my mom and it makes me feel better.

After we finish cleaning everything up, my dad looks over and says, “So I saw Shane talking to you before you got on the bus last night.”

I nod. “Yeah, I ran into him the other day when I went to get us subs and then last night. He was just letting me know he was there if I needed to talk or anything.” I’m leaving out about lunch, I’m not sure how I feel about it yet so no need to get Dad riled up about it.

“I hope you don’t plan on taking him up on that offer.”

“No. I think he was just being nice.”

He blows out a breath that, coming from anyone other than my dad, would sound obnoxious. “Yeah, I’m sure that’s what it was.”

“Come on, Dad, give me a little credit. I’m not going there again.”

He nods. “Okay. I hope so because I won’t be as calm this time.”

I glance at the floor. “I know, Dad.”

He claps his hands together. “Now. How much money did you spend on ski clothes?”

I laugh with a snort. “Billions.”

“Really? Well there went your inheritance.” He makes a *poof* sound with his mouth.

“Nah. Mine and Grant’s were only two hundred dollars.” He gives me a *what the hell* look. “Anne said she’d pay you back. She had me looking because you know what Grant would pick out. Plus, it saved us a pile on shipping.”

He nods. “Okay then. That doesn’t sound too bad.” He reaches out and messes up my hair. “I’ve had a great time tonight, Raven. I mean that.”

I give him a smile. “Thanks, Dad. Me, too.”

Grabbing my phone, I send Shane a text.

ME: I’m sorry, I appreciate you asking but I can’t go to lunch with you. I don’t think this

would be a good road for us to go down again. Thanks for being a friend though.

Shane: Whatever.

Shane: Probably for the best anyway.

Me: I am serious though, thanks for being so nice to me after my mom passed away. I just don't want you to think I want anything more than friendship and the lines between us seem to always get blurred.

Shane: It's all good whatever.

Whew. Okay, that's over. I honestly figured I would get cussed out. That would've been his go-to before. Maybe he has changed.

Not really, I get a text every day. They seem like casual texts but with Shane, I'm waiting for the other shoe to drop.

CHAPTER 14

Grant-

The end of the season flies by with the girls going out in the next round and us just after that. Now we get to celebrate, by going to Colorado skiing. Just FYI, I've only seen snow a handful of times in my life. Each time there wasn't that much. A few times it did manage to snow where we live, we're up close to Tuscaloosa so it's not like being on the coast. Then one year it snowed while we took a family vacation to the Smokey Mountains. Everyone tells me this place is totally different, though.

Plus, I have to say I'm excited at the idea of spending almost a week with Raven. Maybe having some time with her, I'll be able to get my head straight about us. Everyone, and I do mean everyone, even Coach O has asked me about kissing her at the end of that game. I really didn't think that many people would be paying attention to us.

I stuff the last of my clothes into my bag, just as my dad steps into the room. "You ready to go, son?"

I shoulder my bag. "Yes, sir."

I glance over at the clock and see that it's almost ten o'clock at night. He's dropping Raven and I off at the gym where we're meeting the Atwoods and the bus at eleven. I guess since it's a twenty-hour drive, they have two drivers going, to drive through the night and most of tomorrow. Warren had to go out of town on business, so Raven is leaving her car here. She should be pulling in any minute. I follow him out to the truck after kissing my mom bye.

We stand by the truck, waiting on Raven. "Now, we're trusting you to go on this trip. The Atwoods are good people, but they can't watch all of you at one time. Colleges are already watching you and showing a little interest. You're only a sophomore so this is a big thing. Don't go up there and do something stupid in the snow." He levels his eyes at me. "Or out of it. You hear me?"

"So basically don't break anything and don't knock anyone up. Yep, I got it," I say with humor.

"Don't be a smartass, Grant. I'm being serious," he counters, clearly getting pissed.

I quieten down. "Yes, sir. I know, I'll be careful."

Before anything else can be said, Raven pulls into our driveway. She gets out of the car, running around to her trunk. I haven't seen her smile like that in a long time. She grabs her suitcase, slamming her trunk. I step over and grab it from her, she's practically bouncing. "You excited?"

"Yes. I'm super pumped about this trip. I was a little worried about leaving Dad, but him having to go on this trip works out great. I mean it's the first trip he's been on since—" She takes a deep breath. "So, you ready?"

I laugh. "Yeah, I'm not quite as pumped as you, though." We climb in my dad's truck with me in the front and Raven in the backseat. "Oh, by the way, Raven, Dad said don't break anything or get anyone pregnant while we're gone."

She starts laughing. "I'll make sure I keep that in mind. Note to self...make sure I wear a condom or use the more reliable pull-out method." Enter smartass Raven, folks.

"Damn it, Grant," my dad bellows from his seat.

"Hey, I was just giving her the same lecture you gave me," I defend.

"I should just beat your ass before you leave," my dad says as we pull into the gym parking lot. He keeps grumbling about my damn mouth and me not taking shit seriously. Raven is giggling in the backseat.

He pulls into a spot and Raven's door flies open before we even get completely stopped. She's out and hugging Jo. Dad shakes his head, laughing as he grabs her suitcase and hands it to me. He tips his head toward Raven, clearly over our discussion in the truck. "It's good to see her smile and be happy, isn't it?"

I smile and grab my bag, hoisting it up on the other shoulder. "Yeah, it is."

Once the parents get some information from the Atwoods and give us all one last hug, we load the small charter bus. It holds like twenty people, so we're pretty much gonna be doubled up most of the way. We're trying to make sure Mrs. Atwood has a whole seat to herself so she can stay stretched out. I see Clem jump in the seat beside James, *maybe there is something to her and him. Hmm.*

Raven sits across the aisle from Jo and Collin. I stop by the seat. "Let me in."

She smirks, "Who says I want to sit with you? You'll probably fart on me the whole way." That gets us laughs from a couple of the people sitting around us.

"We've basically got twenty hours on this bus so I'm sure we'll be moving around."

"Fine, but you're sitting on the aisle." She slides over to the window. As soon as I sit down, she puts her pillow on my shoulder and lays down. "And I'm sleeping on you."

I roll my eyes. "Like I've ever been able to say no to you."

Soon we're on the interstate heading west. The thump of the road puts most of us to sleep. We wake up as they're pulling into a truck stop with a restaurant attached. Mr. Atwood stands up. "Okay, kids, we're stopping for breakfast while they refuel. Come on in."

We all stretch and groan, standing up, and make our way off the bus. "Where are we?" Raven asks.

I glance around, "I don't know." Everything around us is flat.

Collin smiles, wrapping his arms around Jo's waist from behind. "We're just east of Oklahoma City. So about halfway there."

I nod. "This place is flat."

He laughs. "Yeah. Come on, let's get inside and grab a table."

Once we make it inside, I hear Jo and Raven talking about James and Clem. "I just wish they'd come out and tell me."

"Maybe they're worried you'll be mad," Raven whispers back.

Collin puts his hand on Jo's shoulder. "Quit worrying about it. They'll tell you when they're ready."

She finally nods and takes a seat in a booth with him sliding in behind her. Rave and I slide in on the opposite side. "So have you guys been skiing before?" I ask.

"I have, but Jo hasn't. Dad has an instructor coming just for us. He figures not many people know how to ski."

I laugh and nod. "He'd be correct."

We all order some breakfast and talk about what's going on the next few days. Raven and Jo get up to go to the bathroom while we wait. Right after they leave, Raven's phone dings. Thinking it's her dad, I swipe the screen. I see it's from Shane. I don't open it, I just see what pops up on the preview. Him asking her to meet him for dinner one night this week.

I'm so damn pissed. She told me she was going to stay away from him.

After we eat and get back on the bus, I want to bring it up, but I don't. She and the girls move so they can be closer to talk and I talk with Collin and the rest of the guys while we cross the rest of Oklahoma, through part of Texas and New

Mexico, where we stopped at a roadside diner for supper, then right on into Colorado. As we pull into the lodge, she smiles over at me. “This is going to be so much fun.”

“Yeah.”

“What’s wrong?”

I shake my head and roll my lips in. “Nothing, just ready to get off this bus.”

She nods, looking out the window. “Okay. Good thing we’re here then.”

As the bus pulls to a stop, I stand up. “Yep. Good thing.”

CHAPTER 15

Raven-

I don't know what happened after breakfast but he just shut down. For the last ten hours he's barely said anything. Maybe I'm putting too much thought into it and he really is just tired. We gather in the lobby/common room of the main lodge. Mrs. Atwood stands in front of us. "Okay, now I know from everyone's parents they all had talks with you guys about being on your best behavior. So you know there will be a curfew and no room hopping. I am six months pregnant and I better not have to get out of bed at night and chase you out of each other's rooms. With that being said," she smiles, "I've put you all in rooms with the help of my sons and Joelle. Here's the list along with your room number. The caretakers told me they'd be back in the morning with breakfast at seven so that we can get you guys headed out to ski by eight or eight-thirty. So you guys try to be ready to go when you come down for breakfast. The instructor will be meeting us outside the ski resort office."

She lays a list on the counter. Jo skips over to me, she's already told me we're rooming together. Clem and Vivian are in the room next door and her sister from eighth grade, Janae, and one of the girls from Brock's grade are on the other side. Collin and Grant are in the same room, which I'm sure has to do with the fact that if Collin and Jo want to hook up, she doesn't want to have to sneak around her brother. She figures Grant and I will be the safer bet. Grant only makes general conversation the rest of the night, leaving me to really wonder, *What the hell?*

I stop him before he walks into his room at the end of the night. "Hey, can we talk for a minute?"

He shoves his hands in his pockets. "Yeah. What is it?"

"Did I do something at breakfast this morning?"

He looks at me weird. "No, why?"

"Well, you've pretty much shut down after that. You have barely said anything to me," I say quietly.

"Look, I don't know what you're thinking, but nothing is going on. I'm sorry if you aren't the center of my attention all the time."

Wow, that hurts. "Okay. I was just making sure I didn't do anything to make you mad. I'm probably just tired. I'm going to bed."

"Rave."

"No, it's okay. I'm going to bed. Goodnight." I get into my room and shut the door before crying. Luckily Joelle is still hanging out downstairs with Collin. Laying in the bed, I stare at the ceiling. Maybe I've been misreading his language. He's probably just been nice to me because of losing Mom. He feels like it's his duty or something. I just need to distance myself tomorrow and the rest of this trip.

The next morning after breakfast, we're headed to the ski resort. After we arrive, we meet Kyle and Leah, our instructors. They're not much older than us. Probably college students. Kyle is very hot.

I lean into Clem. "Jesus, do they just build guys that hot out here in Colorado or what?"

She whispers back, "Obviously. Damn, look at that hair."

Joelle whispers, "That body. Holy snickerdoodles."

Our conversation is interrupted when Collin steps in. "They want us to go get fitted for our skis and get you girls some bibs so you can stop getting your shirts wet from the drooling you're doing."

We all start laughing, Joelle smiles at him. "Are you jealous, Mr. Quarterback? It's not all about you?"

He smacks her butt cheek. "No, but Grant and James were looking like they may kill the guy just for being hot."

I snort. "So, you're agreeing with us that he's hot?"

He nods. "Oh, totally. I'm man enough to admit it." He leans in to whisper, "And being that man is what gets me laid by my super-hot girlfriend."

Jo smacks him in the shoulder. "Shut up or you can forget *that* for a while."

We follow everyone else inside and start getting fitted for our items.

Once we're all fitted, we're back outside listening to Kyle and Leah. They go over some basics with us and have us all practice on a small slope. I have to admit, I have killer leg muscles but they're screaming right now from practicing. Once we've been at it for a few hours, most of us decide to go over to the tubes and have some fun. I follow Jo and Clem to a tube and hear a heated discussion going on. "I wish you would just tell me already," Jo whisper yells to Clem.

"Tell you what?"

"You and my brother are either seeing each other or have some kind of weird friends with benefits thing going on."

Clem's eyes pop open. "No way."

Jo stands with her hands on her hips. "I saw you two last night. You were kissing my brother outside."

Clem seems to be tripping over her words. "I, ugh—I, um."

Okay, clearly I need to find someone else to hang out with right now. "I'm gonna go grab a cup of hot chocolate. You guys have a nice chat."

Clem looks at me like I'm abandoning her and Jo looks irritated.

I go into the small gift/coffee shop, placing my order. I take my hot chocolate outside to a small covered seating area. I stare out across the white fluff covering the ground. "It's beautiful."

"Yeah, it is." I'm startled by Grant sitting down beside me.

"Uh, hey, I was just going." I start to stand but he grabs my arm.

"No, you weren't. You just sat down. I figured you'd be with your girls watching for *hot* Colorado guys," he says with a smirk.

"Well, my *girls* are having a discussion right now that's rather intense."

He looks at me confused. "Huh?"

"Jo is questioning Clem about her and James. She saw them kissing last night," I say with my head cocked to the side a little.

"Oh shit. Seriously?" He shakes his head. "They finally got busted, huh?"

"Yep," I say, popping the p.

He seems relaxed, maybe he was just tired or something. My phone dings and I look at it. Damn it, Shane.

He nods to the phone. "Who's that?"

I shake my head. "Reminder text about an appointment."

He nods. "So James and Clem are the only ones keeping secrets, huh?" He stands up and starts walking away.

I jump up and follow him. "What in the hell are you talking about?"

He spins around, grabbing my shoulder firmly, but not too hard. "I saw his text yesterday."

Then it hits me. Yesterday's annoying text came in while we were at breakfast. I laugh. "Seriously?! That's what your fucking attitude has been about?" I pull away. "He's been texting me for weeks. Okay? Weeks! I don't respond. After you saw him talk to me at the game, he asked me to lunch, I didn't go. He's been texting and asking me out since. If you would've asked rather than assuming, you would've known." I shake my head. "Rather than making me feel like shit and you acting like an asshole."

"I'm sorry, Raven. I just thought—"

I cut him off. "You thought I'd go back on my word about him!"

"Well, you have before, he has a way of getting to you," he says, throwing his hands up.

I cross my arms defensively. "So far he's been nothing but nice since my mom died."

He gets close to my face and I see nothing but anger. "Yeah? Well, ask Collin about how much shit he said in the funeral home parking lot about how he'd get you back just to fuck you. Just to screw with your head again, proud that he has that ability."

I see people starting to stare and I'm getting embarrassed. I feel the heat in my face rising. I know deep down Grant would never hurt me, but I need to get away.

"Screw you, Grant." I start walking away and he runs to catch up, grabbing me and pulling me to follow him into a small covered walkway. He pushes me against the wall and slams his lips on mine. His tongue twines with mine, meeting each other stroke for stroke. His hand slides down my side until it lands on my ass. I moan and that breaks our kiss.

I shove him back, slapping him and pant. "What the fuck was that?"

"Something I've been needing to do for a while," he says, sounding almost breathless.

CHAPTER 16

Grant-

I stand there panting after the kiss I've been dying to give her, trying to read her face. Is she going to run or stay?

It hits me that I just put myself out there to my best friend. I just made a complete ass out of myself. I probably just fucked everything up. Before she can figure out her next move, I make mine. I walk away.

It's not long before we're going back to the lodge. She sits with the girls on the bus, not making any eye contact with me. Yep, I just messed it all up.

The past few days have been tense. I'm avoiding her and she's avoiding me. In other news, Clem and James are out in the open now. Which in some ways makes me feel bad. Clem is with James, Joelle is with Collin and because I couldn't keep my mouth shut and my lips to myself, Raven is hanging out with Vivian and Janae. It's not totally a bad thing, but I know before all of this she'd have rather hung out with me. Plus, this has put a damper on Collin and Jo being able to spend any time alone in either room.

Tonight we're having a pit fire on the back deck, doing s'mores and hot dogs. I'm going to pull her to the side and I'm going to talk to her. We've got to figure this out. The more I keep thinking about how stupid I am, the more I remember that kiss. She was into it. She moaned. She wanted it.

Watching her laughing on the other side of the fire makes me jealous. She's talking with Dallas. I turn to Collin. "If you want, I'll slip out for a little bit tonight so Jo can slip in our room," I say with a low voice.

He looks at me with wide eyes. "You will? Thank you, man. Are you gonna go hang out with Rave? I mean I can sense something is going on with you guys, but I didn't want to step on your toes."

I shake my head. "Just trying to figure shit out, that's all." And I'm going to try to get this shit figured out before we leave here in a couple of days.

He stands up, clamping a hand on my shoulder. "Okay, well I'm gonna go talk to Jo."

I nod and eat a bite of my hot dog as I continue to watch Raven.

A few hours later, most everyone is in their rooms exhausted from another day of skiing. The air in Colorado is so different from home. Most of us are athletes and we still find ourselves out of breath. So everyone has actually been crashing pretty early. I'm in the kitchen trying to kill some time before I go up to Raven's room. Getting a coke from the fridge, I sit down in the living room by the fire place.

A door opening makes me jump. I see the Atwoods coming out. "Is everything okay?" Mrs. Atwood stayed in today, she said she wasn't feeling well.

Mr. Atwood looks at me. "Can you go grab Collin?"

I stand up, nodding. "Sure."

I jog up the stairs to our room, knocking on the door. Collin opens it, sticking only his head out. "Sorry, man. Your dad and mom are downstairs, she looks sick. Your dad asked for you to come down."

"Shit," he whispers. "I'll be down in a sec."

A couple of minutes later, he joins me downstairs. "Is something wrong?"

"I'm taking your mom to the hospital to get checked out. She wasn't feeling well and now she's been throwing up for hours. With the baby, I don't want her getting dehydrated."

He nods. "Yes, sir."

"Everyone should be in bed besides you two. Keep an eye on your brother, don't let him do anything stupid. I'll call you as soon as we know something. You know the caretakers are out in the cottage if you need anything."

"Okay, Dad. Call me soon."

With that, his parents leave. He looks over at me. "I thought for a minute there I was busted."

I let out a little laugh. "I could tell."

"What are you doing down here?"

"I was just chilling out and grabbing a coke before I go up to talk to Raven," I say, sitting back on the couch and drinking some of my drink.

He sits down on the other end of the couch, just as Joelle comes down the stairs. "What's going on?"

He explains all about his mom as she listens. Then she turns to me. "You fixed shit with Raven yet?"

I groan. "No, I was about to go talk to her when they came out of their room."

"You should go now. Talk to her, fix this. Whatever *it* is. I'll stay with Collin and we'll send you a text when we know what's going on with his parents."

Taking Jo's advice, I go up the stairs and knock on her door. She opens it just a little, probably thinking like Collin did earlier. "Hey, what's going on?"

"I'm coming in to talk to you, that's what's going on."

She puts her hand on my chest. "The Atwoods."

"Mr. Atwood had to take Mrs. Atwood to the hospital. She's been sick, he's just worried about dehydration," I blurt out. I can see the worried look coming on her face. "So let me in."

She steps back reluctantly and lets me in. "Where are Jo and Collin?"

"They are downstairs waiting to hear from his dad. Jo told me to, and I quote, 'fix shit with Raven,' end quote," I say, sitting on the bed she's using.

She sits further down the bed from me in her pajama shorts and shirt, she's obviously not wearing a bra. "So what was that the other day? You kiss the hell out of me and then you walk away."

"Look, my feelings about you have always been cut and dry, black and white, but now the lines are getting blurred." I lean back against the headboard.

"Blurred like how?" She sits cross-legged.

I let out a big breath. "Like I want to kiss you all the time. Like you in a bikini makes me hard, like I was jealous of you checking out Ryan Reynolds' ass."

"Oh." She looks around. "Um."

I jump forward and scoot next to her. "I understand if you don't feel that way. I mean we've always just been friends. I'm not sure what this is so I don't want to screw us up."

She levels her eyes at me. "I guess we need to figure it out."

I look at her and her eyes have become hooded. Leaning forward, I press my lips to hers, softly kissing her. Soon, our mouths open and our tongues twist and turn around each other. I feel my pants start to tighten so I push back. "We need to stop."

She looks at me and dips her head. "It's okay."

"What's okay?"

She shakes her head, still looking at her lap. "You figured out that it was just—" She looks up, waving her arms around. "Nothing. It was just a kiss."

I touch the side of her face, making her look at me. "I needed to stop because I'm hard as a freaking rock. You do that to me. All the time."

The innocent look on her face turns me on even more. “I do?”

Reaching over, I grab her hand and lay it over my crotch. “Does this answer your question?”

I expect her to pull away or act shocked but she doesn’t. Instead she leans forward, kissing me and rubbing her hand against my jeans.

Reaching down, I grab the hem of her pajama shirt and pull it over her head. I touch her boob, “Is this okay?”

She nods, panting. “Yes. Keep going.” Before I get started, she pulls my shirt over my head.

Pushing her back, we lie on the bed and I kiss her hard as I rub her body, nearing her shorts. She reaches down with her hand and starts to fumble with my zipper. I pull back. “How much further do you want to go, Rave?”

“All the way,” she breathes.

CHAPTER 17

Raven-

All the way...

"Rave," he breathes. "We can't go back if we do this."

I kiss his shoulder and chest. "I know." I don't feel the repulsiveness or the shame that I felt with Shane. It always felt so wrong, so forced, but this feels so right. Grant makes me feel...*safe.*

Our hands fumble as he pulls my shorts down along with my panties and I push his jeans and underwear down. He grabs his wallet out of his jeans before they're all the way down. After he puts the condom on, he looks me in the eyes. "I should've been your first."

"But you're the one that matters," I say into his neck as he enters me.

Sex with Grant is completely different. It's actually good. Well, I guess it is with my limited knowledge. I mean I'm enjoying it this time. With Shane, it wasn't like this. I never really felt like I was into it. I felt like it was what I should be doing, not what I really wanted to do. This time my emotions led me here, I was turned on and I really wanted it.

Lying there afterward wrapped up in each other, Grant faces me. "Are you okay?"

I nod. "Yes."

"Are you sure? I mean this is a huge thing for us," he says quietly.

"I know it is, but it also feels right."

A knock at the door interrupts us. "Grant." It's Collin.

Grant slips on his boxers and goes to the door while I cover with a blanket. This is the first time since we were kids that I've seen him naked. We were so caught up in everything I guess I missed admiring what was in front of me. He has a very nice ass. They talk quietly for a minute and then Grant shuts the door.

"Okay, so he heard back from his parents. His mom was really dehydrated."

Now I worry about her and the baby. "Is the baby okay? Is she okay?"

He waves me off. "Yeah, they're basically fine. They're just keeping her overnight to get fluids in her through an IV. But when they get back tomorrow, they want to go ahead and head home so she can get some rest."

I nod. "That's totally understandable. Is she going to be okay on the road home? That's a long trip."

"Yeah, he said we'll probably see her up walking more. His dad is going to call him in the morning before they leave the hospital, so Jo is going to crash with him tonight and it looks like I'll be sleeping here." He gives me a sideways grin. "If that's okay with you?"

I laugh. "Yeah. I guess so." I settle back down in the bed as he comes over and slides in beside me. "So this is different than our old sleepovers."

He snort laughs. "Yeah, I'd say so. For one, you're naked and two, I'm having very dirty thoughts about you right now."

I rest my chin on his chest. "Oh yeah? Well, I kinda have to tell you something."

He looks down at me. "What?"

"Your ass is right up there with Ryan Reynolds."

His hand smacks my ass under the blanket. "Thanks. I always knew you thought that."

"Well, I had to do a naked comparison."

"Grant?" I ask.

"Hmm," he mumbles.

"What are we?"

He yawns. "We're us. Let's get some sleep."

"Okay."

Now I'm even more confused about us. I'm lying here wrapped up in his arms, but he just says we're *us* and falls asleep. This is probably our last night being able to do something like this and he wants to sleep. As much as I hate to compare, Shane always wanted a second go if we had time.

What is wrong with me? Was I bad? Does he think he made a mistake? Was this a one-time thing? My mind spins over and over the entire situation. I think about how caring he was before and now he's snoring. Was I just a fuck to him because Collin and Jo wanted to have sex? A way to kill some time? Maybe he felt the attraction to me, but in the middle of sex he realized that it was just some fluke. That's probably it. Ugh, why does life have to be so damn complicated?

I get very little sleep before Jo is coming in the room telling us to get up. She and Collin gather everyone up in the living room to let them know what's going on. We all start packing up to be ready to leave once the Atwoods make it back. Grant has tried to show a little affection this morning but it almost feels forced. He touches my back, my hand, but it's really not much more than before. This is going to be a long bus trip back home.

He sits beside me when we load the bus, I'm not sure if that's more out of habit or because of what we did.

God, this is so confusing. I'm getting on my own damn nerves with all of these thoughts. I need to just sleep, I didn't do much of that last night. "Can you hand me my pillow?"

He smiles and grabs my pillow. "Here you go." He smirks. "Tired?" So cocky.

"Yeah, and I've got a headache. I'm going to try to get some sleep so maybe it'll go away."

Now he looks unsure of himself. Ha ha fucker, now you know the feeling. "Okay. I'll sit with Collin for a little bit so you can stretch out and rest. Joelle is up there with his mom working on some craft thing. When she comes back, I'll move back over."

I nod. "Thanks." I stretch my legs across the seat and look out the window as the beautiful place we've been rolls by. This place is gorgeous; I could stay here forever. White tops the mountains, up into the clouds. They say it's like that up there year round.

Dozing off comes a lot easier than I expected. The only time I've gotten up is when we've stopped for food. I made Clem talk to me the whole time about her and James. Then when I got back on the bus, I went back to sleep. I've missed all of the flat land states we've went through, I just started waking up when I heard someone say we're in Mississippi. Only a few more hours 'til home. Maybe if I can just keep my eyes closed, I'll doze back off.

The sound of Grant's voice almost makes me jump.

"I don't want to mess anything up. Raven is my best friend."

Then I hear Collin. *"Just be honest with her."*

Oh God, I can't listen to this anymore. I make him notice that I'm waking up so maybe he'll shut up. If he's going to back away, I wish he'd just talk to me about it and not share it with Collin first.

He looks up as I stand. "Headache better?"

"Yeah, I'm just going to go use the bathroom." After I go to the bathroom and cry for a minute or two, I compose myself. When I open the door, I see Vivian and Janae are painting their nails. This is going to be weird for me, but I can't go back up there right now.

"Hey, can I join you guys? I love that color," I say, pointing to the bottle in Janae's hand. "I've been wanting to add some color since the season is over."

They both look up and smile. "Sure."

I sit in the seat across from them and Janae starts prepping my nails. When we get back at least I'll have a few days before we have to be back to school. I can figure out how to get past this whole Grant and I having sex thing.

"What's going on? You seem off somewhere else," Vivian questions.

"Just thinking about school next week."

She looks at me like she doesn't believe me, but she'll just take the answer. I see Grant keep looking back at me, he finally gets up and walks back.

"Hey, you coming back up?"

Yeah, I'm not talking about this on the bus with him. "In a little bit, I'm getting my nails painted."

He nods. "Okay." Turning, he walks back up to where we were sitting.

Vivian looks at me and so does Janae. "Can we say sexual tension?" That's Janae.

"What's going on with you two?" That's Viv.

I shrug. "Nothing. Nothing at all."

CHAPTER 18

Grant-

She never came back up front and she ran to her dad when we got to the gym. I've texted her, but she's either ignored them or come back with an excuse about spending time with her dad. So now, I'm going to her house and I'm going to get to the bottom of this shit.

If she wants to go back to being friends, if the other night was too much for her, that's fine, but she at least owes me an explanation.

I know she had shitty sexual experiences before me. That's why I held her the other night. I could have totally gone another round and I really wanted to, but I also wanted to respect her. Plus, there was something satisfying about holding her all night. Even with Tab, sex was just sex; with Rave, it is so much more. It's a commitment like I've never made in my life because she's always been so much of my life.

As I turn the corner, I see her sitting out in front of the Sub Hut. As I'm about to turn into the parking lot, I see Shane sit down at the table with her. *Mother fucker*. She lied to me. I pull over in the parking lot next door and think about waiting, but it's not worth my time. Instead, I pull my phone out.

ME: I never knew you to be a liar Rave, but I guess you are.

RAVEN: What are you talking about? I'm not a liar.

I pull out of the parking lot, going back past the Sub Hut and make sure I hit the gas hard, making the glass pack exhaust I had installed on my truck rattle the windows. Yeah, she knows I saw her now.

ME: Don't worry I won't text you anymore and I won't tell your abusive ass boyfriend we fucked. That way maybe he won't beat the shit out of you.

I turn my phone off and toss it into the passenger seat. Once I get home, I hit up some of my friends and plan a last minute camping trip at one of the state parks.

Maybe I won't run into her ass for the rest of the break and I can figure out how to deal with her at school later.

Sitting around the fire, I'm thankful that it's just a bunch of guys bullshitting.

I look over at James, Joelle's brother and a senior who was awesome enough to find us some beer to bring. "So, did your sister kick your ass for hooking up with Clem?"

He leans back, taking a drink from the can. "Nah. She was pissed that we kept it from her, she feels like we lied. But as long as she never has to choose between us, she says she doesn't care."

"So are y'all like dating or friends with benefits?"

"Honestly we haven't put a label on it. We see each other, we spend time together. We hook up at parties, but she has this weird relationship with Harrison." He shrugs. "So I'm just rolling with it. She's cool, she's not clingy, I get hot ass out of the deal and I'm graduating in a couple of months so I don't really need to get into anything heavy. You know?"

"Did you decide where you're going?"

He nods, taking another drink. "Yeah, State. They offered me a partial football scholarship and then with my academic scholarships, everything is paid for. Plus, I need to get away from here. Well, away from my dad and that damn hardware store."

Everyone thought that James would stay here and go to the community college, then one day take over his father's hardware store.

I guess that changed after his parents split up earlier this year. The whole town was talking about it. That's the thing about a small town, everyone knows your business. His dad had once upon a time been like Collin, the golden boy of football, and then he got injured. We all knew he spent more time in the local bar than at home, I guess his mom finally had enough.

I roll my eyes. Man, I'd love to be going off to college. "I'd like to have a friend to have benefits with."

He snorts. "Well, you do. Don't you? Aren't you and Rave...?" He makes a grinding motion.

"No. It's not like that for us. She's dating some douchebag." I can say that with some honesty, right? We only had sex once and she is back with that jackass, so it's not like we have an arrangement.

"Damn, could've fooled me while we were gone." He stands up. "I'm gonna go see if the bathroom beside that tree is working. Then I think I'm going to go see what naughty pics Clem sent me to look at while I'm here." He grins before turning away.

Rave has text me and left messages, but I've erased them all without reading or listening to them. I don't want her bullshit excuses and lies.

Collin comes over and crashes into the chair beside me. "So, you gonna tell me what the hell happened? Jo said that Raven has been completely removed since we got home." Proving my point more, she's with him and pulling away from everyone. Just like he wants.

"She kept avoiding me. I was going to talk to her and I saw her outside of the Sub Hut, then that douche Shane came up to the table and sat down with her. He'd been texting her everyday about lunch so, I guess she finally went. Good for her. Maybe she'll get enough when he puts her ass in the hospital." I stretch my neck, rolling my shoulders. “She’s been texting and calling, but I’m not listening to the bullshit anymore.”

He gives me a look that says I’m a dumbass. “So you just observed the situation, you didn’t get facts? Has she ever lied to you before?”

“Yes, about him.”

He rests his elbows on his knees, looking at the fire. “All I’m saying, man, is sometimes it’s easy to jump to conclusions.”

“You ever do that with Jo?”

He nods. “Yep, as a matter of fact I almost lost her over it. Just don’t fuck up. She’s been your friend a long time, you don’t want to lose her over this. I mean you’ve told me how intertwined your families are. You need to at least make things easier for you to be around each other.”

I stand up, grabbing another beer from the cooler. “Yeah, I guess. I’m going for a walk.” I walk down the path to the small lake and look through my phone. I’ve erased all communication she’s sent me. I flip through the pictures that I took on our trip. A few selfies of the two of us. She looked happy. Hell, I looked happy. We looked happy *together*.

After I finish my beer, I walk back to our camping area and find that our crowd has increased in size. I see people from our school, Greenville and Monroe. Since all of the schools in the county are out for break, I guess a few people spread the word. Which kinda sucks. I wanted chill time with my friends and now we’ve got more people, girls, guys...this is just turning into a damn party. I look across and see that asshole Shane. If I see her with him, I’m going to lose my shit.

He’s talking to some guys from Monroe. I glance around, searching for her. Good, I don’t see her. A blonde girl walks up to him and he lifts her up, kissing her.

Already cheating. Damn.

I storm over to him. “So you’re just gonna cheat on her?”

He looks over at me, clearly pissed I'm even talking to him. "What the fuck are you talking about?"

The girl who was wrapped up with him pulls back. "You told me you didn't have a girlfriend."

"I don't."

"No, you just have a girl that you knock the shit out of and fuck around on," I growl.

Blondie steps back further, but he has his hand around her wrist. "Um. I'm gonna go."

He shoves her a little. "Fine. Go the fuck on if you wanna listen to this dipshit."

She looks startled and backs up again. I point to her. "I saved you some bruising, be happy."

He steps up in my face. "You don't know shit, asshole."

My chest is pressed against his. "Yeah, I fucking know about you."

"You're just totally pissed that I got that cherry before you did." He laughs. "Or has she let you go there yet? It's normally pretty easy, she knows that she's lucky to hook up with anyone since she's shaped like a fucking man."

"If you can't stand her so much, why don't you leave her alone?"

He smirks and shrugs. "Why would I? It's free pussy and it's mine. I have control, she'll do what I want, when I want it." He smirks and shakes his head. "Hell, she was so desperate for the attention, I could've told her to blow me at half court during the middle of Regionals and she would have done it."

I draw back and punch him in the mouth. "Doesn't feel so good, does it?"

He tries to hit me back but misses. I shake my head. "It's a little harder to hit someone your own size, huh?"

The next punch he lands. We manage to throw a few punches before Collin reaches in, pulling me back and someone grabs him. “Fuck, Collin, just let me finish this. He’s talked shit for the last time. I’m done.”

“Nope, not gonna let you get messed up over this.”

I turn and see Raven who looks mortified from what she just heard. She turns and darts in the other direction. I guess that answers my question as to if she was here.

Cher walks up before I can go find Raven. “Come on, Grant. Let’s go walk it off. Some of the guys are going to make his ass leave. I wish she’d have listened to us when we tried to warn her.”

I let her pull me down the path as I wipe my lip, trying to calm down. “I hate that fucking guy.”

“Yeah, a lot of people do.” She stands with her hands on her hips and moves closer. “Something else is bothering you though. What is it?”

I shake my head. “Just some personal shit.”

She reaches in and hugs me, pulling my head down a little. “Well, I’m here if you ever want to talk.” Since she’s tall, her head is close to my ear.

“Thanks,” I say back in a whisper.

“Good to see it didn’t take you long to move on, since we only fucked. Really glad to know it was nothing special. I guess the crap he said back there was all true.” Raven’s voice cuts through the night air like a damn knife.

Cher looks around. “Raven, this isn’t...I’m just gonna go.”

“No, you stay!” Raven shouts, acting like she’s going to walk away again.

“No, you’re going to stay and we’re going to talk this shit out.” I stalk over to her, tugging her arm. She snatches it back.

“Leave me alone. You’ve already fucked with my head enough!” she yells.

I fucked with her head? Oh, I'm over this shit. "How did I fuck with your head? You're the one who pulled back and then started seeing that," I point back to the party, "douche as soon as we rolled back into town! Considering he was here with another girl and talking about your pussy loud enough for everyone to hear, it seems you've got a real fucking winner."

She shoves me in the chest. "I wasn't going to go back to him! The day you saw him, he just walked up! But you had to show your ass and your ability to drive like a dick through town. And at any rate, you're the one that pulled away!"

I point to myself. "I didn't pull away! You did!" I motion to her.

She throws arms around. "So what the fuck was that on the bus then? *'I don't wanna fuck anything up, she's my best friend.'* You were regretting it as soon as it was over." She turns, walking toward the water and away from camp.

I follow her. "Are you going to let me fucking explain *anything* or are you just going to keep walking away?"

She turns around, walking backward still toward the water. "Oh, like you let me? Well, go to hell." About the time the words are out, she finds a root or something and trips over backward. "Oomph."

I walk over to her and pull her up. "We obviously need to have a damn conversation. Come on. This is getting stupid."

"Ouch."

I stop and look at her. "What?"

"My ankle."

I stoop down. "Here, jump on my back. This can't wait anymore."

I bring her up on my back and continue down the path. Once we get to the lake, I sit her on a fallen tree. "Let me look at your ankle."

I take the flashlight from my back pocket and look at her ankle. "I think I just rolled it."

"Yeah, I think so. Turn a little bit so you can just prop your foot up on the log." She does and I sit on the ground. "Okay. So, where did this all get fucked up?"

CHAPTER 19

Raven-

I look down at him, halfway closing my eyes and swallow, trying not to cry from all of the stress. "Did you regret it right after we had sex?"

"What? Why would you even think that?" From the small nightlight on a power pole, I can tell he looks genuinely confused.

"Well, after we had sex you just wanted to go to sleep. Was I bad at it? I mean I've only been with Shane and it was never that great. Well, not for me anyway." Crap, I'm rambling. "It's just, we had this night of freedom, no adults. Most guys would want to go again." Oh shit, maybe he couldn't. I'm soooo not experienced at this. "Could you not," I motion to his crotch. "You know..."

His face goes through twenty emotions, "That's sure as fuck not the problem." He jumps to his feet and paces around. His white t-shirt clings to his chest, stopping just below the waist of his track pants. "No, you were perfect. I don't doubt that it sucked with Shane because you never should've been with him in the first place. He's a selfish ass, so I'm sure that rolls over into bed. I didn't want you to think that you were just ass. Ugh, this is all so confusing."

"Is that really all? I know I'm not like other girls. I have a boy's body. I play a boy sport. I would totally understand if, you know, I didn't make you..." I point to his lower half again. "You know..." Ugh, God, let me die right now.

He puts his hand up to stop me from talking. "I couldn't let things get weird between us, you mean too much." He steps closer, leaning into my face. "As far as you being like other girls? I think you're sexy as hell, your tits are fucking awesome, your ass is just asking to be grabbed and the fact that I can talk to you about sports is a big turn on. Don't let people stereotype you, it's bullshit." He takes my face, pulling my mouth in and kissing me. He pulls back inches from my face, "The question isn't me not wanting you, it's me trying to respect you. I'm sorry if in doing that I made you feel like you were less than perfect for me."

I breathe hard. "I never planned to get back with him and nothing happened at lunch that day. He came up and sat at my table. Asked me why I'd been avoiding him. I told him that I wasn't trying to be ugly but I didn't really want to talk to him. Then you made an ass out of yourself and he laughed, saying that his job there was done. So you played right into his hand. I think he thought I was meeting you for lunch or something."

He shakes his head. "Damn, I'm an idiot."

"Me, too. All of this could've been avoided had I just talked to you about how I felt. I guess knowing that you're, well, let's just say you've had better experiences, it made me nervous."

He sits down in front of me, straddling the log, and pulls me forward into his lap. I'm forced to put my legs on either side of his waist. I can feel how much he wants me and I feel giddy.

I know how I felt when Shane said he wanted me, even when I felt the evidence, and it was nowhere close to this feeling. My tummy feels all bubbly and nervous.

He brushes my hair away from my face and pulls me close. "You are more important than anyone before. Know that, okay? I don't want to mess this up."

I can't help but grind my hips against him. "You're messing with fire, Rave," he groans.

"Maybe I like playing with fire," I whisper.

He pulls my face to his and our lips meet. "Do you want this, Raven? All of this? Us, sex, dates, the title, everything?"

I nod, quickly tugging his shirt over his head. "Damn, Rave." He starts kissing my neck and playing with my nipple. "You are so damn beautiful." He swings his leg over the log, standing up with me still wrapped around his waist. "We've gotta find somewhere to go."

I look around. "We could go back to your tent."

"Um and have a damn audience hearing you call out my name? No." He keeps glancing around. "There." He puts me down on my feet. "Come on, let's go to that boat shed over there. I think it has a loft in it."

He tugs me behind him into the shed and sure enough, there is a small camping loft in the top.

I follow him up the small ladder. "God, I hope there isn't anything that's going to bite me or attempt to eat me up here."

Once we're standing in the loft, he smirks, "I'm the only thing that will eat or bite you up here."

I throw my arms around his neck and we start kissing intensely. Soon our clothes are removed and we can't get enough of each other.

Later, we're redressing and he smiles at me, tugging me over to him. "You have no idea how sexy I find you."

I laugh. "Oh, I got the idea a couple of times."

"So you see, I have NO problem in that department." We both crack up as we go down the ladder and out of the boat shed.

I follow him to the campsite and see that most everyone has cleared out. I guess we were gone longer than I thought. Collin and James are sitting with Clem and Jo. I give them a short wave. "Hey."

Clem snorts. "Well, it appears the two of you have finally gotten on the same page. Thank God. I'm not sure we could stand hanging out with you guys much longer if you didn't."

Jo chimes in. "Yes, the tension was intense."

"Glad we could help you guys," Grant says gruffly.

He sits down on a stump, pulling me into his lap. I smile. "I'm being serious, thanks for worrying about us. It was getting to be a little too much. I wasn't sure what I was going to do when we went back to school next week."

He shakes his head, tugging me around my waist. "I was already afraid I was going to have to beat someone's ass."

I look at him like he's nuts. "What do you mean? Beat someone's ass for what?"

"Because if we weren't together and you weren't with asshat then Preston was already asking for your damn phone number."

I laugh. "Really? Hmm. Well now, I didn't know Preston was on the table. That may have been a better deal."

He starts tickling my waist the way he did when we were younger. "Say I'm the best pick. Say it."

I'm laughing so hard, I'm about to pee. "Okay, okay, it's you. You're the best pick."

Several of the other guys who were planning on staying look around. "Okay, so what are we up to now?"

Clem jumps up. "Ooh, I have marshmallows and stuff to fix s'mores."

James laughs. "Well go get that shit."

We spend the rest of the night hanging out, making s'mores, making out and joking.

I share the tent with Grant. Collin, who was going to share a tent with him, slept in the back of Jo's little SUV. James and Clem share the tent he brought and I'm not sure where everyone else ended up.

Luckily, I'd told my dad that I was staying with Jo tonight. Jo called her mom and explained that she wanted to stay out here. I guess since James is here, she figures Collin won't be trying to hook up. Ha ha, that's funny.

Monday back at school is weird for me. Grant pulls in the parking lot behind me and meets me as I exit my car. "Hey," he says, pulling me into his chest.

"Hey. So how do we do this?" I ask.

"What do you mean?"

"Well, the only boyfriend I've ever had was Shane and we were never at school together during that time. So how do we act at school?" I ask.

He leans against the car, his truck is parked beside my car. "Well, we hold hands. We don't flirt with anyone else at school. We sneak into the old stairwell and make out every chance we get. Oh yeah and if we're lucky enough to be the last ones left after basketball practice, we hookup in the shower." He wags his eyebrows.

I laugh. "Well, that answers some of the questions I had about why you and Preston were so late leaving practice."

"Nope. He wanted me but I'm not cheap like that," he says with a smirk. Then he leans in, "But for you I'd be willing to act that way for the day."

I slap his chest. "Shut up." I grab my bag. "We need to get inside."

He reaches, grabbing my hand. "Come on then."

As we walk into the hall people stare a little, but not as much as I thought they would. I guess we aren't much of a shock, some people had already thought we were dating anyway.

Once I exchange some books in my locker, he kisses my cheek. "Have a good day. I'll see you between classes. Oh, and I had Mom invite you guys over for dinner. I think we should tell our parents we're dating."

That shocks me. "Really, you think we should tell them?"

"Yeah, why not?"

I take a deep breath. "No reason. It's just...okay, never mind. We'll tell them."

He smiles, leaning in and giving me a deep kiss. "Hudson, unlock your lips from Quinn!" I hear my first period teacher, Coach Fagan, yell.

He chuckles against my lips and then backs away. "Ah come on, Coach. Wouldn't you kiss her if she was yours?"

"I can't answer that question, Hudson. It would sound completely inappropriate and just plain creepy." He chuckles. "Now if you'll let her, she needs to get to my class."

"Yes, Coach." He leads me to the classroom door. "See you in a bit."

I wave, laughing at Coach Fagan staring at him. "Bye."

That afternoon I follow my dad to the Hudson house. Greg is grilling steaks when we get there. I automatically go inside and start helping Anne put the salad together. My mom always did that with her. I wonder how Anne is doing. I know how my dad and I have been handling this, but Anne lost her best friend. I don't know what I would do if I lost Grant.

"So did you have a good time on the trip to Colorado? Grant seemed grumpy when you first got back, but then he was happy a few days later. He must've been tired or something," she rattles as we chop veggies.

"Well, I did have a good time. Oh, you and Mom would've totally appreciated our ski instructor. He was hot."

She laughs and cuts her eyes at me. "That sounds like fun."

"It actually was. Snow skiing is something I never thought I'd do, but it was soooo much fun," I say as I toss the cucumbers into the salad.

"Well, that's wonderful. Your mom would be happy that you had a great time." She smiles, but I can see some sadness behind it.

CHAPTER 20

Grant-

After I help my dad grill the corn and steaks, we come in and place it on the island with the salad my mom and Raven made. I smile at her and she gives me a small grin. My dad and Warren are too busy talking about my dad's motorcycle to notice. I'm pretty sure my mom caught it, though.

"Okay, you guys, fix your plates. I think it's nice enough we should eat out on the patio." My mom looks around. "Don't y'all think?"

We all nod our heads and start fixing our plates. I will say that's another thing that's great about Rave. She's an athlete so she doesn't worry about eating. I've been out with a couple of girls who were scared to eat anything other than salad.

Once we're outside, I look at Raven to see if she's ready for us to tell them. She seems nervous, but gives me a nod.

I clear my throat. "So, Raven and I have to tell you guys something. We aren't sure how you're going to take it," I say, standing up.

They all look at us like they can't breathe. My dad slides his chair back a little, as if he's preparing for something horrible. Warren is gripping the hell out of his beer can.

"Raven and I have started dating. We know this is going to be weird for everyone, but it's taken us a lot of time to work out our feelings for each other. We hope you understand." I let out a huge breath I didn't know I was holding in.

My dad lets out a large snort. "Son, don't start a conversation like that if you wanna live."

Raven and I look around the table. My mom laughs. "We were waiting for you to tell us that Raven was pregnant or something life changing."

Warren wipes his mouth. "I love you like my own, Grant, but I was ready to beat your ass."

My dad motions for me to sit down. "Look, we've all noticed things changing between the two of you. As long as you understand that there is going to be more rules about the time you spend together, I don't think we'll have a problem. That's the reason I tried to have a serious talk with you before you left."

My mom shrugs. "Then when you came back grumpy and Raven wasn't anywhere around, I thought maybe it was a false alarm. Then things seemed to work out after you and the guys went camping." She takes a bite of her salad.

My dad glances at me like he knows more about my camping trip, but before he can say anything, Raven pipes in. "It was a lot for us to figure out. We both kept misunderstanding each other. But I guess while the guys were camping, Grant talked with Collin and at the same time I was spending time with Jo and Clem. All of them kept telling us we needed to talk to each other. So when he got back from camping, that's what we did and like I said, we figured out that we weren't communicating. We just kept jumping to conclusions." Warren and my mom are totally into eating now.

I see my dad relax and start cutting into his steak. "So what rules are going to change?" I ask. "I mean it's not like we have sleepovers anymore."

My mom nods and wipes her mouth with her napkin. "Well, it's just going to be more about your time alone."

Raven laughs. "Um, we don't have time alone. We're at one of the houses with you guys, school or practice."

Her dad looks at her sternly. "Well, I'm sure now you guys are going to be asking to go out on dates."

Raven's face is priceless. That's really the first time that thought has entered her head. "Yeah, I guess we will." She laughs. "I guess this is still taking me some getting used to."

That relaxes all of our parents and they chuckle at how awkward this is for us to navigate.

Warren glances at me. "Her curfew is eleven-thirty. No later. I won't deal with the same crap I did the last time she was dating someone. I'm not saying you would because I happen to know your parents would beat your ass. I'm just making that clear to both of you."

I look him in the eye. "Yes, sir."

My dad glances down the table to me. "Your curfew is midnight. That's only so that you can get Rave home and drive here safely. If you break your curfew or cause her to break hers, there will be hell to pay."

"Yes, sir."

"Now, let's eat. This steak is damn good even if I did cook it myself." My dad winks.

After everyone has finished supper and we've cleaned up, Raven and I go outside to shoot a round.

As soon as we make it to the court, she shoves me. "Oh my God, Grant. You almost got us killed at the dinner table. You totally made it sound like I was knocked up or we got married, something totally bad."

"Well, after I said it the way I did, they were just happy we were only dating," I reply.

"Yeah well, the camping thing almost got us," she says as she starts dribbling the ball.

"You did a great job of covering, though. I still don't know if they completely bought it."

She passes the ball to me. “Check. Well, we’re going to have to be a lot more careful and fun time will be limited.”

I dribble around her and shoot, making the basket. “Yeah, well you’re just going to have to behave yourself around me,” I say. “So, if I make this next basket, are you going to go out on a date with me? I mean a real date. Where I pay and we go to the movies or dinner, something like that.”

She steals the ball and takes a shot, with me blocking it and going up for the rebound. “So, what do you say?” I ask, stepping into her personal space.

“I say what time are you picking me up Friday?”

“Six.”

She grins. “Okay.” Then she knocks the ball from my hands and starts walking toward the house. I run behind her and grab her around the waist.

“That was a low blow and you’ll pay for it the next time we play.” I kiss her on the cheek and whisper in her ear, “You’re sexy.”

“You’re not so bad yourself.” She giggles and turns around in my arms. “See you tomorrow.”

I kiss her deeply. “Tomorrow.”

She runs to her car and I watch her drive away with her dad only moments behind her.

Once I’m inside the house, my mom stops me. “Sit, let’s talk.”

Shit, here we go. I knew this was too simple. “Okay.”

“I’m happy that you and Raven are dating. Seriously.” She puts her hand up. “I know I can’t stop you from doing certain things, but please respect her. I know you both have had experiences before. Hers more unfortunate than yours, I’m sure. Just remember the bigger picture. You both have so much potential.” She takes a breath. “Her mother was my best friend for almost twenty years. We always swore to take care of each other’s children like they were our own. So that’s what I’m doing now. I’m thrilled that you guys are dating but remember, this is high school and you both have a long road ahead of you.

So be respectful of each other and be smart. That's all I'm saying." With that said, she stands up and walks from the room.

Fuck. What am I supposed to do with that? Is she really happy or not happy? Am I an asshole?

"I see you're in deep thought," my dad says from the doorway.

"Oh crap. Not you, too," I say as I fall back into the couch.

He sits on the other end. "So I heard part of your mom's warnings."

"Does she think I'm just going to knock Raven up and leave her? This isn't some episode of *16 and Pregnant*. Raven means more to me than that. She's my best friend." I'm getting ill trying to explain myself.

My dad puts his hand out like he's stopping me. "Calm down, son. She's worried about both of you. I mean what would you do if Raven *wasn't* your friend anymore? If you guys break up, that could very well happen."

"Does no one think we've thought about this? Hell, we had a huge blow up over it. I love her, Dad. We may figure out we're better off friends, but how else will we know?"

I don't give him time to reply, I just stand up and walk out back and start shooting free throws. I figured my mom would be the one jumping the gun to plan our damn wedding, but somehow this all got fucked up.

CHAPTER 21

Raven-

Friday, 5:45 p.m. I think I'm going to throw up. I don't know why I'm so damn nervous. It's Grant. I remember him in his *Thomas the Train* underoos. The doorbell rings. That's a first for Grant at my house, he's always just walked in.

I open the door. "Hey. Why did you ring the bell?"

He shakes his head, but before he can answer my dad pipes in behind me, "Because he was raised to be a damn gentleman. When you show up to the house to pick up a girl, you knock on the damn door or ring the doorbell."

Grant motions to my dad. "What he said."

I laugh at both of them. "Okay, well let's go. I'm freakin' starving."

"Me, too. I was thinking we could go over to Monroe and grab a steak."

I look at him like he's nuts. "At Benjamin's Steak House? That place is too expensive."

"Hey, you don't say that when I'm paying," my dad chimes in with a snicker.

"That's because you make the big bucks."

"We're going to get steak. I want to take you to do something nice like you deserve. Now, after that it'll probably be the Frosty King. Just FYI."

That gets a laugh from Dad and I both. "All right, you two, go ahead. Have fun." I hug my Dad's neck. "Love you, Rave. Be careful."

"Love you, too, Dad. We will." Grant grabs my hand awkwardly and I follow him out the door.

Once we're in the truck, I start laughing out of pure nervousness. "What's going on, Rave?"

I shake my head, trying to calm down. "It's just weird. Well, not weird, but maybe strange would be a better word. I was totally a wreck before you rang the bell. Then I felt like we were standing in front of the judge with my dad. Like he knows that we've already been having sex or something." I start laughing again.

He barks out a laugh. "Oh, well then you'll love the lecture I got from my mom defending your honor after you left the other day. I swear she thinks I'm going to knock you up, give you an STD and bring a stripper home to take to prom."

I laugh even harder. "That's funny."

He pulls out on to the highway to Monroe still laughing. "I wanted to say, 'Seriously, Mom, have I had a string of baby momma's show up I didn't know about?' I honestly figured my mom would be so damn excited that she'd be naming our kids and trying to fit you for a wedding dress or some shit."

I shake my head, trying to control the laughing. "I know. I really thought my dad would be the one to lose his head over it. Damn parents keep throwing surprises our way."

We crack jokes all the way to the restaurant. Once we're inside, I'm still not sure about this place. It's not like it's an over the top formal kind of place, it's just they pride themselves on their steak. They raise their own cattle for the steaks so they're expensive. Don't get me wrong, it's totally worth it and if my dad were the one paying, I'd be all over it. This was one of my mom's favorite places to eat, she might have been tiny but she could pack away a steak. But with Grant paying, I know he worked over the summer but he's got to be running low on funds by now.

"Rave, quit worrying. I have plenty of money. I see the wheels turning in your head. This is special and I know this was one of Tara's favorite places to eat." He pulls me into his side as we slide into the booth.

"I know you worked over the summer, but I don't want you to blow your savings."

"What do I really pay for, Rave? I pay for my gas and part of my insurance. Or when I decide I want fast food. Plus, I've still been working," he explains as the waitress drops off our menus.

"Where have you been working and when do you have time?" I ask.

"I've been doing some computer work for dad. Trying to help him stay caught up on emails, filling out and filing some spreadsheets. Stuff like that," he explains.

"Okay, well I'll order the thirty-two-ounce prime rib tonight," I say jokingly and wink. "I can use the protein."

"I got another way you can get protein," he murmurs, causing me to almost spit out the water the waitress just dropped off.

"Well, well, well, if it isn't Grant Hudson and the girl jock." I look up to see that the devil has come back to haunt us. Ciara Mitchell and her two friends, Karmen and Addison Pope.

Karmen smiles. "Are you two waiting for your girlfriends to come back to the table?"

"Wow, you guys need some original material," I say. Like it's the first time someone has claimed that I'm a lesbian since I like playing ball.

They roll their eyes as Grant asks, "What do you guys want? We're on a date."

Ciara covers her mouth in mock surprise. "Oh, I'm so sorry. I didn't mean to intrude. My daddy brings us here every Friday night for dinner. He says money is nothing for a true quality product. Of course I always just get the salad, I mean I have to keep my body looking like this. Some of us aren't fortunate enough to eat like a horse and be built like a boy."

I twist my lips, trying not to laugh at her. She's really trying to brag about money and her body. "So your daddy, he's pretty pissed with the amount of money he's spent on you for a subpar bitch of a daughter," I say as dryly as possible.

They all suck in a breath and Grant starts laughing. "I was pretty sure that private school you're going to would've held an exorcism for you by now. Or did they and it didn't work? Let me ask you another question. Does pea soup really projectile out of your mouth when the demons come out? Like in that movie?" I say, laughing.

"Look here you..." She's interrupted by our waitress.

"Are you two ready to order?" she says with a smile.

Ciara turns to the waitress, about to start bitching at her but before she can, I start to order.

"Sure. I'll have the sixteen-ounce T-bone, medium, with a twice-baked potato, a garden salad with ranch and make sure we get a dessert menu, please," I say, trying to look as innocent as possible with a nice smile.

Grant looks up. "I'll have the same and make sure you bring that dessert menu." After she walks away to put our order in, we look at the queen Bs. Before I know what's happening, Grant's mouth is on mine. He pulls back a little and smiles. "Fuck, you're so hot."

We hear a unanimous "eww" from them, just before they turn and walk away.

We both start laughing. "Well, that made them go away," I say right before the waitress comes back. She smiles.

"I just want to say I heard what you said to them earlier and your dessert is on me tonight." I'm about to tell her no, but she puts her hand up to stop me. "They come here almost every Friday night and the wait staff take turns taking Mr. Mitchell's table because we can't stand them and he's a little grabby. He's a generous tipper, but sometimes it's just not worth it. You know? But you put them in their place. I'm sure the wait staff could take a pool if you wanted to come back every Friday to help pay for your meal, just so you could tell them off."

We both laugh even harder. "No, sorry. Tonight is a special occasion, but maybe we'll come back for any other special occasions and make sure it's on a Friday just to piss them off," Grant says.

I nod my head in agreement with him.

After she walks away, he smiles at me. "You totally crack me up. You went all in on your order and you pretty much called Ciara Satan."

"I can't help it. She's a bitch who stereotypes me. Which someone has been telling me I shouldn't buy into, so I told her off as quietly and nicely as I could in here. Then when she was going on about eating that damn salad, I wanted to show her that I could eat like a damn man and still keep my figure. The demon stuff was just great improv."

He shakes his head. "You would think after what she did, she would try being a nicer person since she got off pretty much free."

A few months back when all of that went down with Booker and Jo, Ciara was charged as an accomplice. She said she would testify against him and so she got probation and community service. She also had to move to a private school as she couldn't attend Everly anymore and no other high school in the district wanted to deal with her.

"Nope, not her. I really don't like her. The fact that she's had sex with you pisses me off even more."

"Babe, she was a mistake." He makes sure I'm looking him in the eye by moving my chin. "Nothing."

"You make me feel—I don't know. Special," I whisper.

"I plan to always do that if I can."

God, I hope he does. I like this feeling in my stomach. It's like happy, fluttery butterflies.

CHAPTER 22

Grant-

If you were to look up happy, smug bastard in the dictionary, you'd see my picture there. I mean being with Raven is a feeling unlike any I've had before. In some ways it's so hard, but most of the time it's the easiest thing I've ever done in my life. There isn't all the pressure that normally goes with dating someone. She's always taken me for however I am. I sound like I grew a vagina, but she makes me happy.

My parents have finally realized that we both thought about this. We both know that we still have two years of high school and college, and that the likelihood of us getting married and having babies is slim, but we're living for now. She says she has realized a few things and that one of them is that we can be taken from this Earth at any time, so we should live life and do what makes us happy. And we make each other happy.

Leaning against her car, I wait for her to come out of the gym. She's started some new workout regimen, getting ready for a triathlon, so she's been training at the local gym with a group of people planning to do the same event.

She walks out fresh from a shower. Her hair is still wet and she's thrown it up into a sloppy bun. The yoga pants she has on do incredible things for her ass.

"Hey, boyfriend," she says, kissing me on the lips.

"Well, I'll meet you outside the gym anytime if you're going to greet me like that." I let my hands slide down to her ass, pulling her against me. "You look super sexy when you look all sloppy."

"Sloppy?" She shoves back. "You dick. I just worked my ass off."

"No you didn't, thank God. I'm just saying you look cute like this. All relaxed, out of the shower with your hair thrown up haphazardly. It's refreshing." I pull her back into to me and give her another longer kiss. "So what did you need me to meet you here for?"

"I need to drop my car off to have the oil changed," she explains.

"Doesn't Warren do that?"

She fiddles her fingers. "Well, I sorta waited a little longer than I should and he's gone on a trip for a couple of days. I just realized how far over it is and I don't want to chance it. Plus, he'll yell at me if I tell him how far over I went."

I laugh. "Let's stop at the parts store and get the stuff. I'll change it at my house." I shove her on top of her head. "I thought you knew how to change oil. I know Warren taught you."

She dances around like a kid. "Yeah, but I don't want to. I was just going to pay someone and tell him I did it so he wouldn't have to. I forgot I had a super sexy boyfriend that could do it for me," she says, raising her eyes.

I shake my head and laugh. "Damn, Rave. Don't con Warren like that." I tug her hand, walking her around to her side of the car. "Follow me." I give her a brief kiss on the lips before closing her car door.

She rolls down her window. "You know, I just had a thought." She gives me a grin. "You could change the oil at my house. You know where everything is and then I could possibly reward you afterward since Dad isn't home."

I nod. "I like your way of thinking. I'll text Dad to let him know I'm helping you with your car."

After we stop at the local parts store, I follow her home. Pulling her car in front of the garage, she drives onto the ramps I place on the ground. I grab the black container for the oil to drain into, shoving it under her car before I lay under it. I unscrew the plug and start to drain the old oil. While I wait on it, I get up and start getting the stuff out to replace it.

Once all of the oil has drained, I remove the old oil filter and let it drain in the container, too. She hands me the filter with the oil already spread around the seal. "Thanks. See, you totally should've done this yourself."

"Shut up," she says with a laugh.

I crawl back up under the car and replace the filter and the drain plug. After I tighten it, I start adding the new oil. A few minutes later, I'm all finished.

After we get everything gathered up and put in the garage, I touch the end of her nose with my greasy finger. "Damn it." She shoves me away, grabbing a shop rag to wipe her nose.

"Now, you were going to pay the shop, how are you going to pay me?" I say with a flirty tone.

She walks over to me. "I'm sure we can work something out."

"Oh yeah?"

"Yeah," she says just before she hits the button to close the garage door.

A little bit later, we're pulling our clothes back on just about the time we hear a door shut outside. "Shit," I whisper.

She snatches her hair back up in the bun, trying to fix it. "Damn it," she breathes.

We go out the side door of the garage to the basketball court and start dribbling. I wouldn't put it past my mom or dad to be coming over here to check up on us. We almost got busted with our hands in the cookie jar, so to speak.

A minute or so later, no one ever comes around so I slip to the fence and look over. I see that asshole Shane in her driveway looking at our vehicles.

I don't even tell her what's going on, I just start out of the gate. "Can I fucking help you?"

"Oh, so you're hanging out here now. Does Daddy dearest know you're here spending *quality* time with his little tomboy?" he sneers.

"That's none of your damn business," Raven yells, walking in between us.

He laughs. "So I take that as a no."

"It doesn't matter what he knows or doesn't know. This," I point between Raven and me, "doesn't concern you."

"Besides, my father did tell *you* to stay the hell off of his property if I remember correctly, so you need to leave or I'll call him and the sheriff." She stands with her arms crossed over her chest.

He walks back to his truck, mumbling something under his breath before jumping in the truck and peeling out of her driveway. I'm pretty sure I heard him call her a dumb slut, but I don't feel like getting in a fight in her driveway. Plus, the next time I hit this son of a bitch, I don't think I'll quit.

"How long is Warren out of town for?" I ask.

She shakes her head, trying to play it cool. "Just a couple of days."

I point to her house. "Go pack a bag, you're coming to my house."

She laughs. "Yeah, right. They aren't going to allow that since we're dating now."

I cross my arms to mock her stance. "I'm sure they will or you can go stay with someone. But your house is too far off the road for you to be out here alone," I explain as I drop my arms and walk back toward her house.

"I've stayed out here by myself before when my parents went out of town. I was fine," she counters, trying to be headstrong and stubborn.

I stop and spin around, facing her and raising my voice. "Yeah, but I don't like that he fucking came out here. He was up to something."

"I'll be fine." She tries to pacify me.

"Damn it, Raven! You either go pack a damn bag and come to my house or I'm calling Warren myself," I argue.

She stops and stares at me like she's going to bitch at me. I start past her. "I'm not fucking playing, Rave. If you won't pack it, I will for you."

She storms past me, shoving me out of the way. "Fine. Give me a damn minute."

While she storms upstairs to pack her bag, I call my mom. "Hey, honey. Your dad said you were helping Raven change the oil in her car. That better be all that's going on," she warns.

"Mom, seriously, you called me honey and then talked about oil and sex all in one breath. Plus, if I was doing anything, you just ruined the mood."

"Good. I aim to do that," she jokes.

"Anyway, I called because Warren is out of town and that prick Shane just came by here."

"Oh no. You didn't get into another fight with him, did you?"

"No but I was about two damn seconds from it. My point for calling is that I don't want Raven staying out here alone."

"You're not staying out there with her—"

I cut her off. "Will you let me finish? I know I can't, but she's coming home with me. I told her I was sure that would be okay since you're her *godmother* and all." Guilt, it's been working on parents since the beginning of time.

"Oh, sure, you pull the godmother card when you want your girlfriend to come stay at our house," she joshes. "Fine, but—"

"I know the rules, Mom. If I want to have sex with Raven, I can't do it anywhere but under your roof. Oh wait, that was drinking. Oops, I get those confused," I joke.

"Damn it, Grant, I'm trying to be serious."

I get that lecture a lot. They swear I never take stuff seriously. No, it's how I deal with stuff. My mind operates too fast to worry about everything. If I took life as seriously as they did, I'd have to be medicated.

"Yes, Mom, I know the rules *for real.* She has to stay in the guest room. We can't be in a room with the door shut," I say dryly.

"Okay. I'll call Warren and let him know she's staying over. On the other hand, I just want you to know that I am proud of you for looking out for her. I'm going to check the guest room and I'll see you guys in a little bit."

"Yes, ma'am."

Raven hits the bottom stair as I hit end. "Okay, you're staying with us and Mom is going to let Warren know."

She shrugs and slings her bag over her shoulder. "I think you're overreacting, but at least we'll get to spend some time together."

She sets the alarm and locks the door, shutting it behind her. I motion to her car. "Just pull your car in the garage and ride with me."

"Nah, Dad will be pissed if he comes home and I'm parked in the garage. I'll just pull over to the side in my spot." She jumps in her car and moves it over before getting out and locking it.

I've already taken her bag and thrown it in my truck. She gets in and I decide to try and make a joke. "So, you wanna go one more round before we go back to my house?"

"Shut up and drive," she says as I turn around.

CHAPTER 23

Raven-

Walking into his house, I see Anne and smile. “Hey, thanks for letting me stay.” Grant walks past me with my bag, taking it to the guest room I assume.

She hugs me. “Of course.”

I pull back. “I wasn’t scared, but he was freaking out. He was all like, ‘You’re coming to stay or going to someone’s house, you aren’t staying here. Blah blah. I’m a caveman, blah blah, grrr.’”

His mom laughs. “Yes, he’s a little like his dad in that way.”

“He was succeeding in pissing me off.” I sit down at the island in their kitchen. “Then he was threatening to call my dad and pack a bag for me. I’m really here to shut him up.”

She laughs harder as she grabs some meat from the fridge. “Yes. I can see that.” She sits a few other things on the counter. “I thought I’d do stir-fry tonight for supper. Does that sound good to you?” She smirks.

I nod, she knows I love stir-fry. “Sure!”

She and I get started putting the meal together. I miss getting to cook like this with my mom. Anne is a great substitute, though. She drops the meat in her wok, browning it, while I chop the vegetables and set them to the side for her to add. I grab a box of rice from their pantry and sit it on the bar just as Grant comes back into the room.

"Damn it. Are we on a diet or something?" Grant groans.

"Would you please stop cussing at me like we're in a locker room? I am your mother. I'm not stupid, I know how you talk, but you've gotten quite liberal with the words you use in front of me. Now, watch your *damn* mouth," she says, pointing at him with her wooden spoon.

He sneaks up behind her after she turns back to the stove and grabs her around the waist, picking her up. "I love you, Momma!"

She squeals, "Put me down, Grant!"

He laughs, sitting her back on her feet. "There you go, ma'am."

She pops him on the arm just as the door from their garage opens. Greg walks in from work, kissing Anne. "Hey, guys." He grabs my shoulder and kisses me on top of my head like he has since I was little. "Rave, good to see you, heard you're hanging out for the weekend." Grant opens the fridge and takes a drink of milk straight from the jug.

"Yes and I promise not to molest your son in his sleep or anything."

Grant chokes on his milk, spitting it out of his mouth and nose. His dad grabs his stomach, laughing at him. He pats me on the shoulder before walking away. "Good to know, sweetheart, but I don't think you can rape the willing," he jokes.

"All of you, jeez. When did sex become this funny topic among us?" Anne scolds as she points the spoon between Grant and me. "Both of you better behave yourselves this weekend. And Raven, don't be a smartass like my son. One of those is enough for this family, honey."

We all share a little chuckle which gains us another glare from her.

Later, Grant and I settle into the den to watch a movie while his parents do the same in the living room. I snuggle into his side. "You want me to go fix us some popcorn?" I ask.

"Nah, not unless you want some," he mumbles into my hair.

I look up at him backwards. "Thanks for changing my oil today."

He grins. "I got a pretty great thank you already."

"Shut up," I whisper shout.

We both become engrossed in the movie we're watching. A little bit later, I wake up drooling on his chest. I wipe my mouth. "Sorry."

"The drooling I could handle, but you snore like a trucker. That was kind of tough to deal with," he says, yawning.

I sit up and punch him in the stomach. "Ass."

He lets out an "oomph" and pins me to the couch. "That's it." He starts tickling me.

I kick and play fight with him. Finally getting my leverage, I push him off of me but we end up rolling onto the floor. He rolls on top of me again. "You've done it now."

"Oh yeah," I say with a laugh and bite his hand.

We've wrestled like this for years, but this time something is stirring inside of me.

"Ouch, you bit me!" he yells.

I push his face with my hand. He licks my hand. "Gross!" I squeak.

"I thought you two outgrew this," his dad says from the doorway.

"And we were worried about them...you know. They're too busy trying to beat each other up," his mom replies.

"Um, babe, do you remember our wrestling matches in college? That's how Grant got here."

Grant jumps up from the floor. “Oh my God! Don’t say crap like that. I’ll have nightmares.”

While he’s standing there, I decide to get even. Raising my leg, I hook it around the back of his knee and he goes down. His parents are both laughing and I jump up, running to make it to the stairs before he catches me.

“I’m gonna get you, Raven!”

I make it to the top of the stairs before he catches me. We both tumble to the floor. “I’m not making a trip to the ER tonight, you two!” his mom shouts up the stairs.

Finally, he rolls off me and we are both out of breath, lying on our back in the hallway.

I stare up at the ceiling. “I’m glad we can still act like this.”

“What do you mean?”

I sigh. “Just that I was worried things would change so much between us if we started dating. But here we are, and I’m still kicking your ass,” I joke.

“You’re not kicking my ass, but I’m glad, too.”

I stand up and yawn, “Well, I’m going to bed.” I call down the stairs to tell his parents goodnight and pull him up from the floor. He gives me a long kiss before I walk toward the guest room. I feel him follow me and then he yelps. I turn to see his dad turning him in the direction of his room and I laugh.

After changing into my sleep shorts and shirt, I settle in the bed. I’m actually very tired. All the training I’ve been doing is exhausting, but it’s to benefit a domestic violence charity in our area so I’m going to do the triathlon if it kills me.

I feel my body relaxing so I close my eyes and drift off to sleep. Suddenly, I’m jarred awake by the door to the room slamming open. “Raven.”

I bolt up in the bed and see Greg standing in the door. “Get up, sweetie. We have to get to your house.”

I jump up from the bed and start grabbing clothes to put on. “What’s going on?”

"I'll explain on the way, see you downstairs in a minute."

I dress quickly and run down the stairs.

CHAPTER 24

Grant-

As we pull up to Raven's house, the fire trucks and cops are blocking the view. We can see the smoke billowing up though. She jumps out before my dad's truck is finished moving. I follow behind her and we make it to the yellow tape before a cop stops us. "That's my house!" she screams.

The cop puts a hand up. "Ma'am, I understand that but we can't let you past the tape. It's not safe yet."

I see my dad call one of his friends from the fire department over. We walk over to where my dad is motioning for us to come. The fireman speaks to Dad as soon as he walks up. "Hey, Greg. What are you doing out here?"

"Hey, Bill, this is Warren's house and this is his daughter, Raven. He's out of town on business and Rave is staying with us. What happened? Do you know how bad it is?"

Bill rubs his face. "Well, it looks like the only damage to the house was the exterior between the house and garage. The garage and that car," he points to her car, "are a lost cause." He pulls his helmet back on. "We'll know more in the daylight. Investigators will be here in the morning."

My dad nods. "Thanks, Bill. What do we need to do?"

"Honestly, just go on back home and rest. Give Warren a call, I'm sure he'll wanna head back if he can."

My dad nods. "Warren is already on his way back, I called him before we left the house. But you're sure the house will be fine?"

"Yeah, we've got the fire out as far as we can tell and we'll have people here until the investigators get here so it should all be fine."

"Thanks again, Bill, we'll be back in the morning."

Once we're back in my dad's truck, I see the tears on Raven's face. I pull her into my side, "It's going to be all right. Your dad will get you a new car and he'll get over the garage."

She shakes her head. "No, you don't understand. All I could think when we pulled up was that everything I had left of my mom would be gone." Wiping her face, she looks at me. "I'm just glad it's not. I don't care about my car."

The rest of the ride back to my house is silent and once we're home, none of us can go to sleep. Around daylight, Warren comes in. After my mom feeds us, we head back over to their house.

A couple of hours later, the investigator asks to speak to Warren. About a half hour later, he comes back. "Well, it appears that your car," he points to Rave, "was vandalized and then set on fire. Whoever did it ran a gas trail to the garage and ran out, so it got the car and garage. Luckily the alarm system triggered from the heat and called emergency services so they were able to put it out before it did more damage."

My dad nods. "Any evidence on who did it?"

He shakes his head. "Nope, they wore gloves. They have a few tire tracks from the road, but with all of the emergency people pulling up last night before they realized it, they ran over most of them. They asked if I knew anyone who'd do this."

"Shane." His name tumbled out of my mouth.

Raven looks at me. "I don't think so, Grant. He's an asshole, but this could send him to prison."

"Raven, he was standing out here yesterday looking at your car and everything."

She doesn't agree, but Warren takes note. "I'll mention his name to the investigator. He can at least question him." He pulls her into a hug. "Sweetheart, I'm so glad you weren't here when this went down. We'll get you a new car, I can rebuild my garage, but I can't replace you."

She looks down. "I was so scared all of mom's things were gone. That was all I could think." She cries into her dad's chest as he soothes her.

They stay with us until they're cleared to go back to their house. They mainly had to have the insurance company come out to assess and engineers had to check for any structural damage before they could let them go back.

The cops said that Shane has an alibi in the form of his girlfriend and swears he never came out to her house. He denies even coming out there that day, but luckily our parents believe us. I know deep down though in my gut, he had something to do with all of this.

Once we're back at school, everything falls into a rhythm. She's back training, her dad got her a new car, well, new to her, and school is going on day to day.

A few weeks later, we're out on a group date with Clem, James, Collin and Jo. We went to see a movie and now we're doing what everyone in this county does, hanging out in the parking lot. This group of girls go walking by us and I hear one of them say something about *that whore*. We all look that way and the girl smirks, "Yeah, we're talking about you. You're Raven Quinn, right?"

Raven, never one to back down, steps out in front of them. "Excuse me? How am I a whore? Do you even know me?"

The bleached-blonde steps up further. "Yeah, you were fucking my boyfriend last time I checked."

That alerts me. "Um, I'm sorry, I don't know you."

She rolls her eyes. "Not you, handsome. Shane."

"I'm sorry, I haven't been with Shane in months," Raven explains. "And at that time he was supposed to be my boyfriend."

The girl rolls her eyes and looks at me. "You may wanna check into that. We broke up because he was with her a few weeks ago."

Raven is getting pissed. "The only time I've seen that asshole recently was a few weeks ago when I told him to get the hell off my property before I called the cops. So if he's fucking someone else, it isn't me." I notice Jo and Clem have moved in to flank Rave. Girls are weird. It's like they're moving into lynch mob mode.

Clem steps in front, "Okay, so I can promise you my girl hasn't been with him. Especially not when she has this fine looking specimen over here." She points to me. "I happened to see his sorry, abusive, white trash ass in Walmart the other day with some big tit brunette girl. So you might wanna check there and leave my girl alone."

Raven laughs. "Actually, that's probably the same brunette he messed around with on me. You might wanna look into that." She turns around and motions for us to follow. "Let's go. We can hang out at my place for a little while."

I follow her to my truck and we climb in, going to her house with everyone following. Once we get there, she turns on the stereo out by the pool. Her dad had to go into Birmingham for the night, so no one is here. The girls sit around talking, while the guys and I shoot a round. Collin's phone starts ringing in the distance and Jo grabs it.

"Hello?" "Oh, hey. Yes, sir, I am." "REALLY! Oh my God! We're on our way."

She jumps up and runs over to us. "We gotta go, your mom is in labor!" Collin passes me the ball and follows her out to his car, with Clem and James following since they rode with them.

I walk over to Raven. "So what are we going to do? Everyone left us." I wag my eyebrows.

She laughs, lying back on her lounge chair. “Come sit with me.” She scoots over and I lie down beside her.

“So what’s up? You’ve got something on your mind.”

“That shit tonight just pissed me off.” She snuggles into me. “I don’t know what game he’s playing but I wish he’d leave me out of it.”

“Babe, that fucker is messed up. He needs help. I still think he had something to do with the fire here. I don’t think you’ll ever convince me of anything different.” We start kissing and running our hands over each other. “Mmm. Babe, we gotta slow down or else we’re going to be doing something else out here.”

She giggles and just then, my phone beeps. “Shit. It’s time for me to go.” I stand up, adjusting myself and pull her behind me. “Let me walk you in.”

I walk her in and make sure she locks the door and sets the alarm before I leave, after I kiss her goodbye.

After I turn on Highway 6, I notice someone fly up behind me. I speed up a little because their lights are blinding me. A minute later, they’re right up behind me again and this time, I feel them bump me.

“What the hell?”

I try to figure out what’s going on but the next bump sends my truck flying from the road and into the ditch. I try to steer out of it before it spins sideways but I feel it start to go over. It starts to roll and that’s when everything goes black.

CHAPTER 25

Raven-

My cell ringing wakes me up. "Hello?" I murmur.

"Raven." I hear a panicked Anne. "Is Grant with you?"

I shake my head, trying to wake up. I try to make sense of what she's saying. "No, he left so he'd be home by curfew."

I hear Greg take the phone. "He's not answering his phone and he's not home." I finally look at my clock, it's been almost two hours since he left.

I jump up from the bed, snatching clothes on as I talk. "I'm going to start driving to your house and see if he's broke down or something."

"You don't need to be out this late, sweetheart. We'll go look for him."

"No, I'm walking out my front door now." I've already jogged down the stairs and grabbed my keys.

I hear him say something like *okay* before I hang up.

Once I'm in my car, I start driving, looking everywhere. Just after I turn on Highway 6, I see a light off the side of the road. It's a dim light. I look at the highway and see skid marks. I slam on brakes and pull over on the shoulder. I jump out of the car, running toward the light. "Grant!" I fall in the ditch trying to get to the silver truck I now see lying against a tree. "Grant!!!!!" I scream. I hear brakes screech on the road behind me.

"Raven!" I hear Greg's voice.

"Over here!" I yell, my voice breaking with sobs. First my mom and now Grant. No, I can't lose him, too.

Still making my way to the truck, I try to see inside but I can't. The truck is turned up on its side and I can't climb up the door that's in the air. His dad comes down the embankment with a flashlight in hand. "Grant!"

He hoists himself up on the side of the truck and uses the light to look down in the truck. "Grant, son, can you hear me?"

Nothing. "Grant!" I scream.

Greg looks down at me. "Raven, go to Anne, she's in my truck on the phone with 911. Tell them he's not conscious." I take off and run to their truck, falling several times on the way.

"Anne, he's not awake, Greg said to tell them." She's screaming into the phone to the emergency operator. Anne has tears pouring down her face. She grabs my hand and squeezes it, trying to be reassuring to me while we wait.

The clock on the dash says it's been five minutes when a firetruck and an ambulance pull up. It feels more like five hours.

It seems like forever before they're loading him into the ambulance. Anne and I have calmed since they got him out of the truck and Greg is holding it together, putting himself in charge. I run to the doors of the ambulance but I can't see anything.

Greg touches my shoulder. "Rave, lock your car and ride with us."

I shake my head. "No, I can't leave it here. Dad will kill me. I'll follow."

"I'd feel better if you rode with us," Anne says.

"No, I'll follow." I need a few minutes to myself. If I'm with them, I'll lose it completely. Anne's face is just broken. Grant and I have both been driving since we were kids and learned on the backside of my property. He's an excellent driver.

The cops kept asking me if we'd been drinking tonight. Like they automatically assume that since a teen got into a wreck, there was alcohol involved.

Pulling into the hospital, I see them just getting him from the ambulance. I park, pretty sure it's some doctors spot, but I don't care.

The staff takes him straight back. I turn to Greg. "Did they say if he woke up on the way here?"

He shakes his head. "Do you have any idea what happened, Rave?"

"No, we left the movies, everyone came to my house. Mr. Atwood called because Mrs. Atwood had gone into labor. Everyone left except Grant. Soon his alarm went off on his phone, reminding him of the time. He left after he made sure I locked up and set the alarm. He was supposed to text me when he got home, but I guess I fell asleep." I shake my head. "I shouldn't have fallen asleep."

"No, sweetie, this isn't your fault." Greg pulls me into a hug. "We should get you checked out, you're scratched from head to toe from falling so much. Your hands are all cut up."

I shake my head. "No, I'm fine. I'll—I'll just go wash up."

A nurse and surgeon come out to tell us that he's being taken back into surgery, explaining to us that they think he'll be fine, but he has some internal bleeding they need to look into. The nurse stays to tell us how to get to the surgical waiting room. I text my dad and Collin while we go there.

Collin lets me know they're in the same hospital if we need them.

Soon, I look up and Clem is coming in the room with James in tow. "Hey," she says before she sits down. "Have they said anything yet?"

I shake my head. "No, what about Mrs. Atwood?"

"Nothing yet. They said she's dilating, but it may still be awhile. They're monitoring her blood pressure and the baby closely since it's still a few weeks early. Especially after she got so sick in Colorado," Clem explains. "They may have to do a C-section if things go crazy."

James yawns. "We were about to go home, but we wanted to check in on you guys. My sister and Collin are staying up here with his parents and Brock. Clem's dad is coming to get us."

After they leave, we sit around staring at the walls. My dad calls me and I talk to him for a few minutes. He tells me he's coming on home. His trip was only overnight anyway so he's just leaving a few hours early.

A doctor comes out at a few minutes until five in the morning. "He's awake, but we had to remove his spleen, and he also has a few broken fingers. Other than that, he's very fortunate. The EMTs told me what the truck looked like and this could've been a lot worse. I know you guys are dying to see him so I'll let you come back for just a few minutes."

We follow the doctor to a room in Surgical ICU. Once we're inside, Grant smiles at me and my heart melts. His mom and dad hug him first but he motions for me to come over. I try to hug him without jostling him. "I'm so sorry," I sob.

"What are you sorry for?" he whispers, brushing my hair with his good hand.

"I don't know." I sob harder into his chest.

He chuckles. "It's okay. You're all scratched up. What happened?"

I pull back. "I'm fine, seriously. Now with you, what happened?"

"Somebody in a truck came flying up behind me not long after I got on 6. I drove a little faster trying to get them off my butt, the next thing I knew they bumped into my rear-end several times. I fought for control, but I lost it and I remember starting to roll, before it all goes blank."

"Did you recognize the truck that hit you?" his dad asks.

He shakes his head. "The lights were so bright, they blinded me."

"Well, soon the police are going to come by and see you. They'll be asking you some questions," Greg explains.

A little while later, the three of us run home to shower and change. They let us know they'll be moving Grant out to a regular room, but he'll have to stay in the hospital for a few days.

My dad comes back to the hospital with me when I return. As we enter the room, we see a couple of men in suits.

Dad nods. "Grant, you okay, son?"

"Yes, sir. These are Detectives Skinner and Jones."

"Where are your parents? I'm sure they'd want to be here while you're talking to the police," my dad asks.

Grant shrugs. "It's okay, I was just telling them what happened."

"So you didn't notice anything about the truck that hit you?" one of the men asks.

"No. The lights were blinding me. I remember something silver reflecting but that's it," he explains.

They look at him like they don't believe him.

"Can't you get some paint or something off the bumper of his truck to match it and look for other messed up trucks around town?" I ask with my hands on my hips.

They both laugh. "Ma'am, this isn't an episode of CSI or something. It's not that easy." The second guy adds, "We are going to look into everything we can, but we don't have much to go on."

"Fine."

"Grant, did you tell them about Shane Gibson?" my dad asks. The cops look at him as if questioning why he's speaking.

"Shane dated my daughter some time back. He's had a problem letting go, I guess you'd say. There was a fire at our house the other week and it was arson. We suspect him, but we have no physical proof."

"Hmm, that seems like a lot for a teenage boy who is just upset he got dumped."

"He was abusive toward her," my dad tries to explain. "He's shown up at my house uninvited and unwelcomed."

"Well, how come this is the first we're hearing about it? Have you put a restraining order against him or told the police about the abuse?" He directs this question to me.

"Um, no. I didn't think it was that serious to start with, but then he seemed to get more aggressive," I try to explain.

The one officer looks at me with a little sympathy. "Well, then it probably wasn't serious enough to warrant it."

My dad steps forward. "Wait just a minute. I don't like the tone you're taking with my daughter, and I don't think the Hudsons would be happy with you speaking with their minor son, who just had surgery, without them here. If you'll talk to Sheriff Justine, you'll find out I have talked to him about this situation and he questioned Shane himself about the fire at my house. He felt like the kid was lying through his teeth, but there wasn't enough evidence to take him in. We don't live in the city limits so that's why I didn't report it to you."

The two officers nod. "Sorry. We'll be back to talk to Mr. Hudson when his parents return."

They leave and my dad pulls me into a hug before he takes a seat. "Jeez, I gotta quit going out of town. You guys keep scaring the shit out of me."

CHAPTER 26

Grant-

My parents have shown me the pictures of my truck. How in the world I survived and only have the few injuries I have, I'll never know. Rave says her mom was looking out for me. I think it has to be something like that.

She has barely left my side since the accident three and a half weeks ago. She goes to school but comes here right after and stays the night. It's funny, she just bulldogged her way into my house. Her dad finally caved once he figured out that I wasn't up for bedroom aerobics. That doesn't mean when we've had the chance, we haven't snuck in some third base action.

The doctor cleared me yesterday to go back to school, he said my recovery was a record. Probably due to me being an athlete and young. All I know is that shit hurt for a while. I'm still not allowed to do anything strenuous for another two weeks, but I'm tired of being at home. I actually want to go back to school. Everyone has been great with helping me stay caught up on my classes. Hell, a few of my teachers let Rave sit in and video the lessons. Luckily, the broken fingers are on my left hand so I've been able to write.

The only bad part is since I'm going back to school, our parents have called a halt to the sleepovers. Raven has to go home tonight.

After we finish breakfast, Mom kisses both of us goodbye before I follow Rave to her car. "I'm still coming by to get you every morning until you're cleared to drive. Well, or until your parents get you something to drive." She laughs.

I slowly sit in the passenger seat of her car. "Jeez, I wish Warren had gotten you an SUV or a truck. This is so low to the ground."

"Quit bitching. Wasn't it just last night that you were like *'Babe, I can handle it. Come on, let's be quick,'"* she says with a dropped voice, making fun of me.

"Yeah, well maybe if you'd let me, I'd feel more flexible this morning," I say with a smirk.

"Oh, so what I did do for you last night wasn't enough? I'll remember that."

Oh shit. Red alert. Red alert. I'm pissing her off. "I'm joking, babe. You know I'll never complain about what you do for me."

"It's going to be weird going home tonight," she whispers.

I grab her hand and kiss it. "I know. I'm going to miss you, too."

The rest of our day is filled with school and friends trying to catch me up on everything. Collin's mom had a healthy little girl. Clem's softball season is in full swing and they brought back sloppy joe day in the lunchroom. All in all, a great school day.

When we pull into my driveway, I see a dark sedan that just screams law enforcement. My dad's truck is in the driveway so at least there is that. Warren was right, they were fucking pissed those cops came to talk to me without them. They went to the chief, who happens to be Clem's dad, and he was pissed. He also got their asses for how they talked to Raven.

I look to Raven. "Do you wanna come in?"

She nods. "Yeah, for a few minutes. I'd like to see why they're here. And I have to get my stuff."

I open the front door and walk through. “Hey, guys, I’m home,” I call out.

“We’re in the living room,” I hear my mom say.

As we enter, I see two new detectives are here. “Guys, have a seat,” my dad says, motioning for us to sit. “This is Detective Black and Detective Lewis from the sheriff's department. They are now looking into the whole case.”

My mom scoots forward in her seat. “Raven, your dad will be here any minute. They’d like to talk with all of us about some things they’ve found.”

Seconds later, Warren knocks on the front door, opening it at the same time like he’s done for years. They go through the introductions again and he sits by Raven.

Detective Black speaks first. “Okay, after your accident, we questioned Mr. Gibson about it and again about the fire. He provided the same alibi he did before, his girlfriend. Only this time, she didn’t cooperate. She informed us that she was breaking up with him. It seems you guys had an altercation at the movies that same night, Ms. Quinn?” Her dad levels his eyes at her.

Raven nods. “Yes, she approached me and started yelling, she thought I was sleeping with Shane. Words were said, but I did tell her that the person who he was cheating with wasn’t me.”

They nod. “Well, I think she figured that out on her own afterward and says that he asked her to say she was with him on the night of the fire. So we now have some grounds to investigate further and we have obtained a search warrant. We are having some trouble locating him, do you know of anywhere he would go?”

She shakes her head. “No. I never went to his house or anything like that.”

“Okay, well if you think of anything or if you see him, call us immediately.” The detective hands her a card. “That is my direct cell number. Use it.”

“Yes, sir,” she says quietly.

He hands us all a card. "Just in case."

They say their goodbyes and leave. Warren glares at Raven. "Why didn't you tell us about getting into a damn argument the night of the accident?"

She shrugs. "I don't know. At the time it didn't seem that important. It was just some girl running her trap."

"From now on, you share anything that has to do with that guy. Do you understand me, young lady?" he practically growls.

She swallows hard and I see her fighting back tears. "Yes, sir," she whispers.

"Now go grab your stuff and let's get home."

She nods, making her way to the stairs. She glances behind her to see if I follow, but the way they're staring at me, I better not.

"Son, I know you've had a lot on your plate, but how come that wasn't something you shared either?" my dad asks.

"Like she said, it didn't seem like such a big deal. It was some skanky girl being mouthy. Hell, Clem was standing there, too. She told the girl off."

My dad levels his eyes at me. "From now on, anything gets told."

"Yes, sir," I mumble and make my way to the stairs to check on Rave.

I find her packing her duffle bag in the guest room. "Hey," I say softly.

She looks up at me with a sad smile. "Hey."

I walk over and pull her into a hug. "I love you, Rave."

She sobs into my chest. "If Shane caused your wreck, if he's the reason my house was almost burnt down, this is my fault. I brought him into the fold. You should stay away from me. I've caused you enough problems, Grant."

I place my hands on both sides of her face and make her look up at me. She looks so sad, so broken. "Babe, this isn't your fault. You didn't know this about him, you didn't know he'd be fucking coo coo for cocoa puffs. Even if you'd never went out with him, he could've still been stalking you."

She shakes her head. "I just wanted to feel like I was something to someone. I wanted to be wanted. I was so tired of the hurtful things people would say about me. Someone finally thought of me as more than a friend. Thought I was sexy and wanted me. I should've known it was too good to be true."

"Hey, I want you, I think you're sexy as fuck and I don't give a damn what anyone says. It took me a while to get my head out of my ass, but I'm fucking glad I did." I lean in and kiss her deep.

"Ahem," comes from the door. I see my mom standing there.

"Raven, baby, your dad is ready to go," she says.

Rave wipes her eyes. "Okay." She hugs my mom. "Thanks for letting me stay with him." She turns back to me. "I'll be by in the morning to take you to school."

I shove my hands in my pockets. "Okay, see you then."

She goes down the hall and my mom steps in the room. "What was all of that about?"

"I think it was just Raven being angry with herself. She feels like all of this is her fault," I say, sitting on the foot of the bed. "She's upset that I could've been hurt, that she could've lost her house. This all has her stressed out."

Mom sits down beside me and hugs me. It feels like something I've been missing for my mom to hug me. "She was terrified when we got to the wreck. She'd fallen several times trying to get to you and her screams when we pulled up were gut wrenching. I couldn't even get out of the car because I was afraid of what I was going to see. Don't get me wrong, it was bad, but not as bad as she thought it was. The angle that your truck was at, she couldn't see you. Your dad had to jump on the side of it in the air, all she knew was that it was crushed into a tree. I think all she could think of was her mom."

I nod. "She told me since she's been staying here that her mom was looking out for me."

My mom smiles. "No doubt. That's what best friends are for. She knows I'm looking out for Raven, so she looks out for you."

"Thanks for helping me through all of this, Mom."

"I love you, baby. That's what I'm here for," she says, hugging me. "I wish Raven could see her as we see her, but unfortunately the dumb shit people say is what sticks. If her self-esteem had been better, she probably would've never started dating him. It's such a shame people put young girls through so much scrutiny. She couldn't see the beauty that she is, she saw the tomboy people kept saying she was."

I sigh, "I think she's beautiful. I always did, just in a different way."

CHAPTER 27

Raven-

My dad has been distant all night. He gave me the silent treatment all through dinner. He just drank his beer, ate and got up to watch TV.

He's disappointed in me. I get it. I'm disappointed in me. If I'd never went out with Shane, we wouldn't be dealing with this. I need to help put an end to this. I started it, now I need to finish it.

I step in the living room. "Dad, I'm going to bed. I know you're angry with me. I'm sorry."

Before he can say anything else, I run upstairs to my room. I take the card the detectives gave me and program those numbers in my phone. An hour or so later, I hear my dad go to bed. Taking out my phone, I text Shane.

ME: I need to see you.

It doesn't take him long to respond.

SHANE: I knew you'd come back. What happened Mr. Basketball dump you on your ass?

No, but he needs to think he's won.

ME: Something like that. Can I meet you tonight?

SHANE: Sure DADDY isn't going to bust you?

ME: Nope.

SHANE: Come down by the mill. There is a cabin about a mile down the two trail road. Meet me there in an hour.

ME: Okay.

I dress quickly and set up a text with the directions that he gave me. I have it ready to send to the two detectives, my dad and Greg. I call the sheriff's department to make sure that at least one of the two detectives are working tonight so when my text goes through, I know they'll get it.

An hour later, I'm creeping my little car down the two-trail road to the cabin. I would've never known this was back here without him telling me. I wonder if this is where he has been while they've been trying to find him.

When I pull up, I see that it's more of a shack than a cabin. There is a lantern glowing in the window. I send the text to the group. He opens the door after I pull up and I walk toward him. "Hey," I say nervously. I keep ahold of my phone in my pocket, hitting the button to make it record just before my foot hits the small step to go in.

"So what do you need, Raven? You need some dick because Mr. Basketball won't give it to you?"

"Shane, why do you keep trying to hurt us?" I shake my head. "I'm trying to understand. I thought you loved me at one point."

If he thinks I'm caving, maybe he'll talk.

"What do you mean hurt y'all? You're the one who threw me away like last week's garbage. Just like my parents." Oh, he's trying guilt.

"I broke up with you because you cheated on me and you put your hands on me."

His face turns red. "I don't have to explain my actions to you. If I want to fuck someone else, then you're supposed to stand by me. Men have a lot stronger sexual appetites than women and since you could hardly see me, I had to satisfy it somewhere. Instead of breaking up with me, you should've been trying to figure out how to spend more time with me and please me better." He steps forward and closes in on me. "As far as me putting my hands on you, I needed to keep you in line. Most women need that."

"Who told you that? Women don't need to be kept in line," I snark back.

He puts his hand in the middle of my chest and pushes me back into the wall. "I did. My mom is a worthless bitch but at least she knows not to talk back to me." Holy crap, does he hit his mom?

"Why can't you just leave us alone? You've already moved on. Why try to burn my house down or run Grant off the road?"

He gets close to my face. "Who says I did those things?"

"I know you. You did it," I say, breathing hard.

"Well yes, to punish you." He leans in and bites my neck so hard, I cry out. He pulls back. "Just like your parents took you away from me, I tried to take things away from you. Maybe you wouldn't be so high and mighty if that nice car and two-story house you live in was gone along with everything else. And Grant, I just hate that son of a bitch. He doesn't know how to mind his own damn business. He needed to be gone. You think he loves you? You're wrong, he feels sorry for you. He probably laughs at you behind your back. He tells his other whores what a sorry fuck you are." He tugs me by my hand to the door. "Now, you get to stay with me."

I keep glancing around the room. I expected someone to be here by now. I'm so fucking stupid. I should've brought some kind of weapon in with me. I shouldn't have come out here. "What? Why?" Now we're on the porch, is there anything here? I see some firewood.

"Because you caused my alibi to break up with me. I know the cops are looking for me. She told them I lied. So you're coming with me. We're leaving town." He's pulling me harder toward his truck but I pull back.

"Let go," I growl.

"No. You're coming with me. You don't want Daddy to have to bury his little girl right beside her bitch mother, do you?" My feet lock down and stop moving.

"Did you...? Were you the person who hit my mom?" I choke out.

He laughs. "No, but I wish I would've been. She'd deserve it for trying to keep us apart."

I see red, that's the only way to explain the strength I get to pull away from him. I try to run to my car but he grabs my hair and pulls back. "You're not going any fucking where but with me."

I sling an elbow back, hoping to connect with something, and I end up hitting his chest. "No, I'm not." I pull loose, I'm sure leaving part of my hair in his hands. I get to the porch and grab one of the pieces of firewood, throwing it at him. I'm not sure if it hits him or not. I run into the shack, slamming the door. There's no lock. I start looking for something to block it within reach, but no such luck so I brace myself against it. He starts slamming into the door until I can't hold it anymore and I'm thrown to the floor. He's over me before I can crawl away. He flips me over and I kick him, connecting with his ribs.

"Bitch!" I try to scurry backward to stand up but before I can, he reaches down, grabbing my hair and punching me in the face. "Stand up."

He pulls me up by my hair. "I fucking hate you! I wish I would've never met you."

He stops moving. "Why would you say that? I love you."

"Shane, let me go," I try to say calmly.

"I can't do that," he says in words that almost sound like a sob. "They'll take you away." He reaches to touch my face and I flinch. "I really am the only person who can love you like this." He seriously believes this. "You make me so angry. You make me do all of these things, mean things. Why won't you listen?!" he yells.

I hear cars roaring down the little road now. Thank God! "No. Here they come. We have to go." He pulls me but before we can get outside, cars with red and blue lights come screeching up. He slams the door of the shack and grabs a chair to brace against the door. Sure, he has more time than I did.

"Shane, let me go and I'm sure they'll get you some help," I say, trying to calm him down.

"No. You're mine. Don't you understand that? I didn't say we were over. You said it and that doesn't matter. I'll eventually forgive you for cheating on me, but only after I've punished you." Holy shit, he's cracking.

"Shane Gibson! This is Detective Lewis with the sheriff's department! Is Ms. Quinn with you?"

"Yes!" I scream.

"Raven!" I hear my dad yell.

"Daddy!"

Shane shoves me to the floor. "Shut up."

"Shane, we need to know that Raven is safe," the detective calls out.

"She's fine! We're leaving as soon as y'all move."

"Shane, we can't let you do that, unless she says she wants to go with you."

He pulls me up from the floor. "Tell them you want to go with me and that you love me." I don't say anything. "Tell them!"

"I can't," I sob. "I don't' want to go with you."

"Shane, I'm Detective Black. You need to let her go now. If we have to come in there, it could get dangerous and we don't want that. We wanna get you some help."

Shane keeps trying to peek out the small window. In doing so, he's loosened his grip on me. I try to break loose and run, but as soon as my arm is loose he grabs it again. I shove him, knocking him into the small table. The lantern falls to the floor, shattering and catching an old blanket on fire. He snatches me with him as we fight, me trying to get loose from him. The fire is spreading, but he's determined not to let me go. I start coughing, I can't breathe. "We have to get out of here, Shane," I choke out.

"No. We'll just die in here together."

The smoke is getting thicker by the second. This place must be made out of lighter wood. I hear a crash behind me and I'm knocked once again to the ground. I feel the back of my head and feel warm goo. I fight to stay awake but darkness takes over.

I start to feel like I'm being dragged, but I can't seem to open my eyes.

The next thing I smell is antiseptic and I hear beeping.

CHAPTER 28

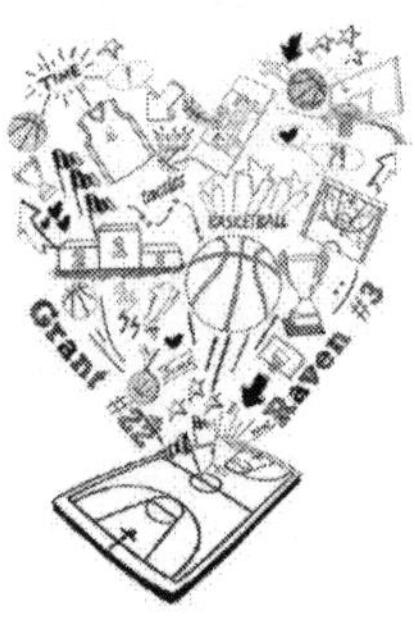

Grant-

"What in the hell do you mean she went after him?" I yell at my dad who is running to his truck.

"You stay here. You shouldn't be straining." He tries to push me back in the house.

My mom grabs me from behind. "Grant, get your ass back in this house!"

My dad is in his truck and gone within seconds. "Damn it, Momma! Give me your keys."

"No! Go sit your ass on that couch. He'll update us when he can," she orders.

I sink into the couch with a deep ache in my chest. My mom sits beside me, trying to calm me. "When I get ahold of that girl, I'm going to beat her ass," she says firmly.

Waiting. Waiting. Waiting. That's what I spend the next hour doing. My mom's phone rings, breaking us from the craziness.

"Hello...oh God...okay, we're on the way." She turns to me. "Get your shoes on, we have to get to the hospital."

"What happened?" My heart is pounding. I feel like it may tear out of my chest at anytime. I can feel tears welling in my eyes, but I won't let them loose.

"Long story your dad said. He said he'd explain when we got to the hospital. Raven was burned, not too bad, but she inhaled a lot of smoke and was knocked out."

I get in the passenger side of my mom's SUV as she races to the hospital. We're both quiet and scared.

Once we arrive, I run into the ER, not even checking to see if my mom is following. I see the cops and our dads. "What happened?"

They explain to me what they know, which is mainly just the text Raven sent and how once they got there, it was like a hostage situation. A lantern was knocked over and started a fire. By the time they got inside, a beam had hit Rave in the back of the head and knocked her out. It burned part of her back while it was lying on her.

I look at Warren. "What in the hell made her decide to go looking for him?"

He shakes his head. "I don't know. I intend to find out as soon as I can."

"Where is that asshole Shane?" I growl. I wanna kill him.

Dad steps forward. "They treated him for minor burns and took him to lockup as far as I know."

A couple of hours later, the doctor comes out and greets us. Warren tells him he can talk in front of us. "She has mainly first and second degree burns across her shoulder blades, but there are a couple of spots that are third degree. We had to place some stitches in her head where they said a beam hit her. We're going to be giving her breathing treatments for the smoke she inhaled. Her right cheekbone is fractured from what looks like a fight, I don't think it was the fire." He looks at the tablet he's using to look over his notes. "She'll be moved up to room three-ten in about twenty minutes. I'll let you visit for a few minutes but then she needs to rest and visiting hours are technically over. A nurse will come out and get you when she's settled."

My fear is now settling and I'm angry. Why would she do this? Why would she put herself in this much danger? I look up at the ceiling. "What in the hell was she thinking?" I level my eyes with Warren's. "I'm not going to lie, I'm so damn mad at her right now."

He rests his hand on my shoulder. "I know where you're coming from, son."

My mom steps in between us. "You two will not go in there charging like damn bulls. She's been through hell tonight and those burns aren't going to be all better by morning. You can ask her some questions, but if you turn into assholes I'm going to make you leave." Warren goes to say something but she puts her hand up. "I know you're her dad, but Tara would say the exact same thing. Let that baby rest tonight, she's probably feeling bad enough about her decision right now as it is. Trust me, I want to beat her ass myself, but now is not the time."

We both take a step back. My mom may be tiny compared to us, but she can get hella scary.

Warren nods. "I guess you're right." He sits down, dropping his head into his hands. "I think that may be the reason she did this in the first place now that I think about it. Right before she went to bed, or told me she was going to bed anyway, she said something. I was about half asleep in front of the TV. I heard her say something about knowing I was angry with her and that she was sorry." He looks up, locking his fingers together and resting his chin on them. "I could've lost her tonight. Just like her mother, I could've lost her." I hear him choke up.

I look around at anything but him. If I look at him right now, I'll lose what little bit of composure I have left. I have kept my damn tears in check. I can't lose it now.

A nurse comes out to let us know that she's been moved.

My mom grabs my shoulder. "Come on, let's go upstairs and check on our girl so we can head home."

Once we're in her room, the nurse explains that she's been hooked up to IV antibiotics and fluids and that her burns are dressed and she has to keep them covered right now. She doesn't have a top on, but they have the sheet tucked under her arms to keep her covered. Her face is bruised and I can see her hair is burnt. She's been through hell on Earth.

She opens her eyes and starts to cry. "I'm so sorry, Daddy."

He walks over to her side and gently kisses her head. "I know, baby. Eventually you're going to tell me what the hell you were thinking, but right now you need to rest."

He looks to my mom and she nods, happy that he's controlled himself.

My dad gives her a jokingly hard time about causing so much drama before he steps back. I look at her and she starts crying harder. "I'm so sorry, Grant. He did it. He hurt you on purpose because of me." She sobs.

We're all caught off guard. "What?"

"Where's my phone?" she asks. "I need to give it to one of the detectives."

My dad steps out and asks the nurse. The nurse brings in a bag with Raven's things in them. They find her phone in the bag and hand it to her. Detective Lewis is still in the hospital and comes to her room as soon as her dad calls.

Once he comes in, she hits play and our world is turned upside down. We hear firsthand what happened from the moment she stepped foot in that shack until her phone must have cut off the recording when she was trying to get out during the fire.

Holy shit...

Everyone in the room, with the exception of the Detective, is crying.

He looks at her sternly. "Young lady, you did a very brave but stupid thing. I know you probably realize from the pain you're in how bad you screwed up and I appreciate you trying to help us get him, but never, never, never do something like that again. I have a daughter close to your age and I'd lose my mind if something like this happened."

She nods. "Yes, sir. I honestly figured everyone would be right behind my text."

He shakes his head. "Sweetheart, this isn't like cop shows on TV. I was on the other end of the county when the text came in. It's a miracle I made it as fast as I did. What would've happened if your dad had gotten there first? Hmm? It could've gone really bad."

"Yes, sir. Trust me. I kept thinking the whole time I was there just how stupid I was. You don't have to worry about me doing something that stupid again," she says, twisting her hands together.

"Good. Thank you for what you did. I don't want you to think I don't appreciate it, but from now on just let us do the police work," he says before patting her leg. "Get better." He briefly speaks with Warren before leaving.

After hearing that recording, I'm still angry, but I think she's punished herself enough.

I walk over to her and kiss her forehead with tears rolling down my cheeks. I'm not even trying to be manly and suck it up because I can't.

I could've lost my best friend, my girlfriend, my other half since birth tonight. I tuck her head into my neck and whisper into her ear, "I love you, but if you ever do anything like that again, I swear on everything I have, I'll spank your ass."

She giggles with a snort from the tears and I pull back and kiss her hard on the lips. I don't care that our parents are in the room. She grabs my hands. "I love you, too, and I'm sorry."

EPILOGUE

Raven-

It's been four weeks since I decided to play cops and douchebags. My burns are healing, but they hurt. I'm having to do whirlpool therapy, which sounds like fun but is actually like having salt poured in an open wound.

After I get out of the therapy tub is when the true torture begins. They have to clean the wounds and dress them, which hurts so bad.

I'm going back to school, I just can't carry my backpack or get sweaty.

It's okay, Grant has been sweet. I guess he's trying to make it up to me for taking care of him, but I still feel like this whole thing is my fault. Anne suggested to my dad that I start seeing a counselor to help me deal with some things.

It's been great to go in and talk about my mom, the mess with Shane and my feelings about myself and my looks. I've only just started, but it feels great to have a place where I can just vent and be honest. I'm sure there will be days that I hate it, but in the end I know it will be worth it.

Right now Shane is being treated in a psychiatric facility. They have doctors checking to see if they think is competent to stand trial for the crimes he's committed. I have very mixed feelings about it all. I listened to him that night. There were times I thought he actually believed what he was saying. I do feel like he needs some help, but I'm not sure he's not responsible for what all he did.

A knock on my bedroom door breaks me from my thoughts. "Are you ready to go?"

I smile at my dad. "Yes."

It's Grant's birthday and his parents have planned a surprise party for him. All kinds of food, a D.J. and all of our friends. It's here at our house because it's warm enough to use the pool and our patio is huge. Plus, when my dad rebuilt the garage, he added a man cave. Why he thought he needed a man cave when I'll only be here for a couple more years, I'll never know. I guess he always wanted one and he finally got it. So he's got the Braves game on in the cave.

"So what are you telling him you guys are doing?" my dad asks before I get in my car.

"Just going out, but then you are going to call me and say you need me to come back here for something." I shrug. "He's already offered to take his dad's truck, but I insisted on my car." I look around, trying to think if we've forgotten anything. "Everyone does know to park behind the fence so he can't see them, right?"

My dad nods. "Yes, and Greg and I will be out here directing."

I sigh. "Great. Okay, I'm going to go. Call my phone and give me a fifteen-minute window."

He kisses my cheek. "All right."

An hour later, my dad is making the call to me and I put him on speaker. "Hey, Dad."

"Rave, I know you guys are on a date, but I think I left the alarm off. I need you to run back to the house and check it. I'd do it but I'm on a schedule and I don't want you going home tonight and it not being on."

I look over to Grant who is driving my car. "Yes, sir. We'll run back there now."

Once we pull up in my yard, I'm glad to see that nothing is out of place. "Can you come in with me? I just don't like going in alone if the alarm is off."

"Sure, babe." He wags his eyebrows. "Maybe you can give me my birthday gift while we're alone."

Shit. "Maybe later. I'm all dressed and I don't want to get messed up."

He follows me to the front door. As I open it, the lights are out. Before I can set the alarm, he pushes me against the wall and starts kissing me. "Baby, do you know what I want for my birthday? I'd love to have your—"

"SURPRISE!!!!" everyone yells. His mother's face is flushed, our friends are snickering, my dad looks like he may throw up and Greg is trying his best not to laugh.

"Oh my God, guys!" he yells. "You got me."

We follow everyone out to our pool. "You didn't have any idea?" I ask.

He laughs, shaking his head. "No, you totally pulled it off."

Hid dad clamps his hand on his shoulder. "We'll talk about what you and Raven are doing in your spare time later. Right now, I need you to follow me." We follow his dad to the back side of our garage where the basketball court is.

When we round the corner, there is a brand new Chevy Duramax sitting there with a bow on it.

"Holy shit!" he screams. His hands are shoved into his hair with his mouth gaping open.

His parents had told him they would help him get a newer truck after the wreck. He bought the other one, but they decided to get him this one as a surprise. Apparently the plan was to get it for him when he turned eighteen, but he's getting it a year early.

All of our guy friends are crowded around the truck doing guy things, oohing and ahhing.

He runs to me, picking me up and spinning me around, then hugging me and kissing me. "I love you. I can't believe you kept this from me," he whispers in my ear. "I may spank you for that later."

I laugh. "I love you, too."

He shifts, throwing me over his shoulder. "Let's go for a ride." I squeal as he carries me to the truck.

He sits me in the seat and kisses me hard.

My mind runs through all of the things I've been through in the past year. The good, the bad and the horrible.

I once read a quote in a book that makes so much sense at this point in my life.

It's that time in your life when you start to find yourself. When you get your heart broken for the first time. When what's happening after "the game" is more important than anything else...except maybe this kiss.

A SERIOUS NOTE FROM THE AUTHOR

This book touched on subjects close to my heart. Teen dating violence, domestic violence and body image among the biggest.

- Roughly 1.5 million high school boys and girls in the U.S. admit to being intentionally hit or physically harmed in the last year by someone they are romantically involved with.
- Teens who suffer dating abuse are subject to long-term consequences like alcoholism, eating disorders, promiscuity, thoughts of suicide, and violent behavior.
- 1 in 3 young people will be in an abusive or unhealthy relationship. The tricky question: what does an unhealthy relationship even looks like? We've created a guide to help you spot the signs. Pre-sign up for 1 in 3 of Us, launching May 1!
- 33% of adolescents in America are victim to sexual, physical, verbal, or emotional dating abuse.
- In the U.S., 25% of high school girls have been abused physically or sexually. Teen girls who are abused this way are 6 times more likely to become pregnant or contract a sexually transmitted infection (STI).
- Females between the ages of 16 and 24 are roughly 3 times more likely than the rest of the population to be abused by an intimate partner.
- 8 States in the U.S. do not consider a violent dating relationship domestic abuse. Therefore, adolescents, teens, and 20-somethings are unable to apply for a restraining order for protection from the abuser.
- Violent behavior often begins between 6th and 12th grade. 72% of 13 and 14-year-olds are "dating."
- 50% of young people who experience rape or physical or sexual abuse will attempt to commit suicide.
- Only 1/3 of the teens who were involved in an abusive relationship confided in someone about the violence.
- Teens who have been abused hesitate to seek help because they do not want to expose themselves or are unaware of the laws surrounding domestic violence.

Sources

1 The NO MORE Project. "Dating Abuse Statistics." www.loveisrespect.org. Accessed April 22, 2014..

2 USA.gov. "Teen Dating Violence." Centers for Disease Control and Prevention. Accessed April 22, 2014..

3 Liz Claiborne Inc and The Family Fund. "Teen Dating Abuse 2009 Key Topline Findings." http://nomore.org/wp-content/uploads/2014/12/teen_dating_abuse_2009_key_topline_findings-1.pdf

4 The NO MORE Project. "Dating Abuse Statistics." www.loveisrespect.org. Accessed April 22, 2014.

5 Decker M, Silverman J, Raj A. 2005. Dating Violence and Sexually Transmitted Disease/HIV Testing and Diagnosis Among Adolescent Females. Pediatrics. 116: 272-276.

6 The NO MORE Project. "Dating Abuse Statistics." www.loveisrespect.org. Accessed April 22, 2014..

7 Hattersley Gray, Robin. "Dating Abuse Statistics." School Safety. http://www.campussafetymagazine.com/article/Dating-Abuse-Statistics (accessed April 22, 2014).

8 Hattersley Gray, Robin. "Dating Abuse Statistics." School Safety. Accessed April 22, 2014..

9 Chamberlain PhD MPH, Linda. "Dating Violence Literature Review." Futures Without Violence. Accessed on April 22, 2014..

10 Hattersley Gray, Robin. "Dating Abuse Statistics." School Safety. Accessed April 22, 2014..

11 Hattersley Gray, Robin. "Dating Abuse Statistics." School Safety. Accessed April 22, 2014..

12 USA.gov. "Teen Dating Violence." Centers for Disease Control and Prevention. http://www.cdc.gov/violenceprevention/intimatepartnerviolence/teen_dating_violence.html (accessed April 20, 2014).

If you need help or are hurting, please find help. Listed below are some contacts for help.

<u>Crisis Text Line</u>: Text SUPPORT to 741-741 (24/7). Our trained counselors can discuss anything that's on your mind. Free, 24/7, confidential.

<u>Depression & Suicide</u>

The Trevor Project Call 866-488-7386 (24/7) Live Chat with the Trevor Project (Fridays 4:00 PM to 5:00 PM EST)

<u>Dating Abuse & Domestic Violence</u>

loveisrespect Call 1-866-331-9474 (24/7)

Chat Online with loveisrespect (7 days/week, 5:00 PM to 3:00 AM EST) or text **loveis to 22522**

National Domestic Violence Hotline Call 1-800-799-7233 (24/7) Email the National Domestic Violence Hotline (24/7)

RAINN: Rape, Abuse and Incest National Network Call 1-800-656-4673 (24/7) Live Chat with RAINN (24/7)

Domestic Violence is a pattern of behavior used to establish power and control over another person through fear and intimidation, often including the threat or use of violence. Other terms for domestic violence include intimate partner violence, battering, relationship abuse, spousal abuse, or family violence. Domestic violence and abuse can happen to anyone, regardless of gender, race, ethnicity, sexual orientation, income, or other factors. Men are victims of nearly 3 million physical assaults in the USA. One in four women will experience domestic violence during her lifetime. ** (www.safehorizon.org/page/domestic-violence, n.d.)

From my personal experiences. It's very easy for someone on the outside of a relationship to say what a victim should do or what they would do if they were in said relationship. The truth is no one but the victim can make these decisions. Most of the time the victim cannot think past what has been put into their head. "You're not good enough, No one else will want you, You're sorry, You're ugly, You're fat, You'd be alone if it weren't for me." Comment's like those are common. The goal is to isolate the victim and make them feel as if the abuser is the only one they have in their life. If you or someone you know is the victim of domestic violence, please find help.

10 SIGNS OF DOMESTIC VIOLENCE AND ABUSE
Some signs of domestic violence and abuse are more obvious than others. Below are a few of the most common signs of domestic abuse and violence.

Does your partner ever:

1. Accuse you of cheating and being disloyal?
2. Make you feel worthless?
3. Hurt you by hitting, choking or kicking you?
4. Intimidate and threaten to hurt you or someone you love?
5. Threaten to hurt themselves if they don't get what they want?
6. Try to control what you do and who you see?
7. Isolate you?
8. Pressure or force you into unwanted sex?
9. Control your access to money?
10. Stalk you, including calling you constantly or following you?

If you recognize the signs of domestic violence and suspect that you or someone you know is in an abusive relationship, you are not alone; there is help in your community.

Call our domestic violence hotline at **800.621.HOPE (4673)** or 311 in New York City. If you're a domestic violence victim outside of New York City, call **800.799.SAFE (7233)**.

If you suspect that you are experiencing domestic violence or relationship abuse, remember:

- You are not alone.
- You are not to blame.
- You *do not* deserve to be treated this way.
- You have rights.
- You can get help.

If you suspect that someone you know is experiencing domestic violence or relationship abuse:

- Get Information.
- Get Resources.
- Go to www.safehorizon.org

(www.safehorizon.org/page/domestic-violence, n.d.)

The subject of body image with Raven comes up quite a bit. Myself being born at 10lbs, 11oz and 23 ¾ inches tall, I've always been a bigger girl. I woke up in the seventh grade one morning and couldn't see my feet anymore because of the big boobs I sported. I was taller and broader than most of my friends. Growing up with friends who were all single-digit sizes was at times humiliating. Guys loved staring at my boobs, but didn't realize that a size zero body didn't go with them. So many times wanting to be the one chosen and not was hurtful. It took a few wrong decisions to find my way. The point is I found my way and although I don't think I'll ever be completely comfortable with my body, I've learned to accept it and move on. Someone loves me for who I am. Someone likes my big ass and large boobs and it doesn't matter that I'm not a single-digit size.

My point is love yourself for who you are, whether it's tall, short, skinny or thick. You have to love yourself first. Someone is out there who will love you for all of your imperfections and quirks. Just love yourself first.

Thank You,

S.M. Donaldson

Acknowledgments

Thank you to my readers. Without you, I would not be having this awesome adventure. You have helped make my dreams come true and for that, I'm truly blessed and grateful. I'm happy that many of you have embraced the idea that I needed a little break from the deep stuff. Going back to high school was somewhat refreshing.

To my family, thank you for being supportive. Special thanks to my mom who listens to the endless ramblings about my characters.

I need to give a big Thank You to Chelly Peeler. She's not only my editor, but my friend. She always listens to my random crazy thoughts. She loves my characters and understands my craziness. Thank you again.

To my bestie, Chelsea Camaron, thank you for being my sounding board. Thank you for giving me those little bits of advice, for helping me think three books ahead. For not thinking my random late night texts are crazy or annoying. For understanding my need to format as I go and not laughing too hard at my attempt to outline the rest of the series. Love you. #commentbubblinbitch #blurbbitch

To Kimberley Foster Holm for treating my books like Where's Waldo and helping me find those little things that I've read over a hundred times. #warnagirl

Thanks to my PA Shawna Powell. I just don't know what I would do without you. You are always up for a challenge and I wouldn't have gotten this book done without you taking care of social media so I could write. XOXO Big hugs.

To Ena and Amanda at Enticing Journey Book Promotions. You guys have given me the best experience with promotions ever. Love you girls.

To Melissa at Indie-Vention. You just get it, what else can I say? I send you a little info and you go to town. Love this cover. Thank you so much.

~S.M. DONALDSON~

Thanks to all of the book bloggers out there who spend so much time helping us promote books and everyone who leaves a review, you are all awesome.

To my street team, Donaldson's Dirty Debutantes, and everyone in S.M. Donaldson's Reading Room you guys are just awesome. I don't know what I would do without you.

To my Author friends, thank you for being supportive and inspirational all at the same time.

About the Author

S.M. Donaldson is a born and raised Southern girl. She grew up in a small rural town on Florida's Gulf Coast, the kind of place where everyone knows your business before you do, especially when your Daddy is a cop and your Mom works for the school system. She married one of her best friends at the age of 20 and has one son. She is a proud military wife, has always had a soft spot for a good story, and is known to have a potty mouth. At the age of 31, she decided there was no time like the present to attempt her first book. Sam's Choice was born and she hasn't stopped since. If you are looking for a good, steamy, Southern set romance with true Southern dialect, she's your girl.

My Links:
www.smdonaldson.com
www.facebook.com/s.m.donaldson.author
www.goodreads.com/AuthorSMDonaldson
Twitter: @SMDonaldson1
Instagram: SMDONALDSON1981

~S.M. DONALDSON~

Other titles by S.M. Donaldson

New Adult Titles

The Sam STRENGTH Series
Duet Available
The Temptation Series
Box Set Available
The Secrets of Savannah Series
Box Set Available
Novellas
Just the Other Sister Series
(E-book only)
Seasons of Change Novella Series
Summer of Forgiveness
Falling for Autumn
Holiday with Holli
Camilla In Bloom

Adult Titles

Marco's MMA Boys
Lesson For Lox (Short Story)
Letting Lox In
In Sly's Eyes
Holding Huck's Heart
Gaining Gibbs
Crazy Christmas (Short Story on Insta Freebie)
Jacob Exposed
Sergio Spiraling (Novella)
Sergio's Redemption (Coming Soon)

(Young Adult Titles)
Game Time Series
Crimson Catch
Guarded Heart

Tutus & Cowboy Boots

Part 1

By Casey Peeler

Chapter1

Cadence

I grab my dance bag and toss it over my shoulder. Laura, my best friend and duet partner, walks out of the dance studio behind me.

"So this is it," she says with sadness in her voice.

"I guess so. What am I going to do without you?" I ask as she embraces me. "I mean why did my dad have to do something so stupid? And why am I the one being punished for it?" I ask as we pull apart.

"Just promise me if you have a chance to come back home, you will. I don't know how you're going to survive out there in the middle of nowhere. Do they even have cellphones?" Laura questions.

"Yeah, I'm sure they do but who knows if there will be any signal in the middle of a field. Well, I better get going. I have dinner tonight with Dad and his home-wrecking secretary. Maybe if I put on a smile, he'll change his mind."

"I got my fingers crossed," she says while holding up her hands. I smile, but deep down I know better. My father is a selfish son-of-a-bitch. Not only did he mess around with his secretary, but he didn't even put up a fight for me so tonight is our goodbye dinner. I know Laura wants me to come back, but it will never happen. I just hope and pray that my future isn't as bleak as I envision it.

As I walk into our spacious apartment, I quickly drop my dance bag in the laundry room and hurry to get ready. Dad moved out six months ago and now this house is cold and all my memories that made it a home are all distorted. I knew Mom would sell it eventually, but I wasn't prepared for her to move out of the city. And we're not just moving to the suburbs, we're moving to fucking Hillbilly USA. Never in my life did I think my mom would resort back to her Southern roots. She always told me she left for a full-ride to NYU and she'd never move back. When she met my dad, I'm betting she didn't see this in her future. Tomorrow morning, we're loading up our new Suburban, also known as our peace offering from Dad, and heading south to Delight, North Carolina. I can tell you right now, there's nothing delightful about that town.

I check the time on my phone and have exactly fifteen minutes to catch the subway to get to Dad's on time. I arrive at the station with five minutes to spare. As I stand waiting on the platform, I wonder if he's going to do something special tonight. Oh! Maybe he's changed his mind and will ask me to stay. I continue to ponder the possibilities as I take my seat. At exactly seven o'clock I knock on Dad's door and am greeted by the home-wrecking bimbo. I smile as sweetly as possible, but underneath I want to take my nails and mess up that pretty face and rip out that bleach-blond hair. She lets me know Dad is in his office as I step into the apartment.

"Hey Dad," I say as I lean on the doorframe.

"Hey Cadence. How was school and dance today?" he questions like he genuinely cares.

"It was great! I had so much fun telling everyone goodbye," I say sarcastically.

He pauses and looks at me. "Don't be like this. You're leaving tomorrow. Can we please have a pleasant night?"

"Of course," I say as I turn to help the bimbo set the table.

Dinner is the same routine it has been each week since he moved out. I try to convince him to let me stay here and he gives me the same bullshit about needing time with the bimbo, and making their relationship work. I want to scream, what about our relationship? I'm your favorite girl. At least that's what he always said. I guess he lied.

When we finish eating, I leave my dishes on the table. That bitch can clean them her damn self. Dad asks me to sit on the patio with him. He makes small talk for a few minutes, and then I know what's coming. Goodbye.

"Cadence, I really wish things were different, but your mother believes that going to Delight will be best for you. I agree."

"What about what I think? I've lived in New York my entire life. Do you really think that I'm going to be able to fit in, in that spec of a town? Not to mention it's my senior year. I have some amazing companies looking at me. Dad, everything is done. I need to be with Lauren. We've already choreographed our senior piece. How am I going to find a partner, learn a new piece and find a decent school? These are big name companies. They don't want someone from some little hick town. You sent me to these schools because they were the best. Do you honestly think the best are in Delight, North Carolina?"

"It will work out."

"Right, just like you and Mom." I stand. "I guess I need to get home so I can finish packing," I say as I stalk toward the door.

"Cadence, don't do this. I don't want you to leave like this." I start to laugh as I turn to face him.

"Funny thing is. You didn't think once about me and how I felt when you put our family second. Bye Dad." As I open the door, he calls to me.

"Cadence!" I take in a deep breath and stop in the doorway. "No matter what I love you. Just remember that." I nod.

"Love you too Dad," I say as I close the door. It's true because no matter what, he's my dad.

Walking up to our building, I see every light is on in our apartment. I take a deep breath. I don't want to cry. I want to be mad. Mad at my dad who doesn't want me and mad at my mom who is taking me away from everything I've ever known. I check my reflection in my camera app to make sure no tears have escaped then make my way inside.

"Cade, is that you?" Mom asks as I pass her bedroom.

"Yes," I say hurrying to my room. I don't want to talk right now.

"How did it go?"

I laugh. "How do you think?"

I kick off my shoes, and Mom walks into my room as I begin to remove my jewelry. "That bad, huh?"

"Oh, best time ever, Mom," I scoff.

"I'm sorry," she says as she pulls me into her arms. I refuse to cry in front of her.

"It's okay. I don't need him."

"Actually, it's not. As much as I want to say you don't need him. I know that he's your dad, and you do. Things will change. Just give it time." I nod. "Now, you need to go to bed soon. Tomorrow is going to be a long day. The movers will be here at eight."

"Okay. Night Mom," I say.

"Love you, Cadence."

"Love you, too."

□

Chapter 2

Cadence

"Cadence." I hear my mom's voice as she knocks on the door. I pull the covers over my head. "Cade. It's time to get up," she says. I hear my door creak open and know I have no choice. It's time to face reality. My life, as I know it, is over. Feeling a dip in the bed, I wait to hear what she has to say next.

"Honey, I hate this as much as you do, but it's what's best for us. Gran is willing to let us stay with her until we can get on our feet. Who knows maybe you'll even like it there," she says as she pulls the covers back. I pull my pillow on top of my head to keep out the light. "Seriously, Cadence. We don't have much time. The moving crew will be here soon." Knowing there are only a few items left to move, I get out of bed. "That's my girl. Come on. Once they finish up, we'll be on our way."

I put on something fashionable yet comfortable for our ten-hour ride to Delight. Pulling my covers off my bed, I quickly fold my comforter and say goodbye to my bed. I might have to say goodbye to it, but there's no way in hell I'm leaving my Lilly Pulitzer comforter. That's out!

Walking toward the foyer, Mom stares at me. "What?" I ask.

"You know we can buy a new one," she says.

"Yeah, but this is mine, and I'm not leaving it," I say.

She shrugs her shoulders, and brushes it off. We take the remainder of our personal items and place them in the Suburban. Thankfully, Mom has shipped most of our clothes and valuables. We are taking a final look around the apartment when the movers arrive. Not only is Mom selling the apartment, she's selling all the furniture. She said Gran has everything we need for now so it's not worth taking it with us. Gran's idea of décor and this place are polar opposites so I think Mom is crazy for not wanting to keep our stuff. When I pushed her to keep some of it, she grumbled something about not wanting any of his crap as a reminder. It all just sucks and Gran's house is a time warp to the sixties with god-awful country flair. It would be nice to have some pieces to remind me of home.

After the trucks are packed with the rest of our stuff, we decide to stop by my favorite bakery for a flavored coffee and fresh baked croissant for breakfast. As Mom drives out of the city, I quietly eat my breakfast and we make small talk. After we merge onto the interstate, she cranks up the radio and sets the cruise control. I text Lauren until she has to leave for the studio, and wish I was going with her.

Barrick

I roll out of bed before the rooster crows, slide on my worn out jeans and shirt, and then grab my boots and head toward the kitchen. Sitting my boots by my chair, I open the refrigerator and grab the orange juice and drink straight from the carton.

"Barrick! You know better," Mama says as she hands me a glass.

"Sorry, but it taste better this way," I admit.

"You sure it doesn't have to do with not wanting to do the dishes?" I shrug my shoulders. "What time you think you'll be home tonight?" she asks as she twists her hair into a funky knot on the top of her head.

"Probably four. Ms. Brown said she wanted to stop a little early today."

"Are you serious? That doesn't sound like her," Mama says.

"Yeah she's got family comin' into town." Mama doesn't say anything, but I can tell by her stance that she's thinking about something. I finish my juice and slide on my boots. I slide my worn out ball cap on my head, pick up my truck keys, and grab a fried apple pie on the way out the door.

Arriving at the Brown's farm, I pull my truck alongside the barn and notice the lights are on. Walking inside, I see Ms. Brown filling the feed buckets for the horses.

"Mornin' Ms. Brown," I say.

She stops and turns to me. "Boy, I've told you to quit calling me that! It's Mae Ellen or Mae, but not Ms. Brown. Now, grab that feed and get to moving. We got a lot to do today, and not a lot of time."

"Yes Ms. Mae," I say.

"That's better," she says as she continues to work.

I spend most of the morning with the dairy cows. I swear I've seen more cow milk in the past two months than my entire life. Who would have thought that a farm in little old Delight could be such an asset to our county and the foothills of North Carolina? When Mr. Brown passed away three years ago, my older brother, Bo, helped Ms. Mae. Now that he is overseas with the Marines, she asked if I'd like to help. I had no idea what this job actually entailed.

After lunch Ms. Mae asks me to do a few things out of the ordinary. This woman's got me carrying boxes, mopping, and even wants me to go the grocery store for her. The only time she's ever asked me for help inside was to fix a broken door handle. I don't ask any questions, I say yes ma'am as she gives me each task. She must really be excited about her family coming into town.

As I set the groceries on the table, I hear her holler for me to come help her upstairs. When I make my way into the room, I hurry a little bit more when I realize she's struggling to move a dresser. I quickly grab the other side, and we both move it with ease.

"'nything else Ms. Mae?" I question.

"Nah, I just got to make the beds and I think I'm about finished. You've been such a big help 'round here. Thank you."

"No problem," I say as I help her neatly stack boxes in the corner of the room.

Glancing at her watch she informs me it's a little after three. "Go ahead and call it an early day Barrick. I'm going to finish up here and then relax a little bit."

"You sure?" I question.

"Yeah, just be here at normal time tomorrow."

□

Chapter 3

Cadence

Staring out of the passenger side window, I can't help but wish my life were different. The farther down the interstate we drive, the faster my dreams fade behind me. Who knew that one act—or hell, maybe more—by my father would impact my life to this extent? I cannot stand him.

Hearing my phone beep, I take my phone from my purse. Touching the screen, I see a picture from Lauren. It's a selfie of her in the studio with a pouty face. I smile knowing that she's missing me, but seeing the studio makes tears well up in my eyes. I quickly wipe them away, grab my ear buds and turn on my favorite playlist.

Mom and I make fairly good time, but I'm so tired of being in this vehicle. We stop every few hours to stretch, use the restroom, and get a snack. When we hit the North Carolina state line I get excited, but my excitement is quickly extinguished when I realize we still have a few more hours to go.

As the sun begins to set, the light is blinding as we drive west on interstate forty, but once it's behind the trees we're no longer squinting behind our sunglasses. We make a turn off the interstate and Mom calls Gran to let her know we're almost there. She says that she has dinner waiting for us, and I can only imagine what varmint she's fried up.

As if she's reading my mind Mom looks at me. "Stop it. You know she's not going to feed you something crazy."

"You never know, but I bet no matter what it's something fried and a million carbs," I say with attitude, and Mom pulls the car off to the side.

"Look, I left Delight thinking I'd never go back, but sometimes we can't control what happens in our lives. I know that this isn't want you want to do right now, but I didn't want a divorce either. As much as you think your life is over, it's not. Take a moment and think about me Cadence. I've lost everything I've worked for and your father. The least you can do is be grateful that Gran is letting us move in with her. Now I'd appreciate you putting a smile on your face when we get to Gran's just like I'm going to do."

I don't say anything because if I did she'd probably make me walk the rest of the way to Gran's and there's no way in hell I'm walking out here by myself.

Mom drives in silence as I stare out the window. We finally arrive in Delight, and when I say we've arrived I mean we've passed a tiny green rectangular sign with the word Delight on it. There's no post office, shops or anything. It's a spec of a community near an extremely small town called Lawndale where there isn't a chain restaurant for thirty miles.

Turning onto the gravel driveway I see the glow of the lights in the farmhouse. Once Mom puts the Suburban in park, I open the door and almost vomit from the stench that invades my nose.

"What is that smell?" I ask as I hold my nose.

She starts to laugh. "Cadence, it's the country, but more than likely that's a bunch of cow manure."

Oh. My. Gosh. I woke up in New York and landed in hell. I quickly grab my essentials and as I begin to walk toward the house, I trip over something. I squeal and catch my balance. "Why's it so dark out here?"

"Cadence, honey, this is the way God made it. There aren't any street lamps. Just give your eyes a moment to adjust." I do and it helps, but before I take another step, I grab my phone and turn on my flashlight. I then drop my essentials on the ground.

"No service! Mom! My phone has no service!"

"You'll survive. Gran has a landline." Who the hell is this lady and where did my mother go? Shoot me now!

Want more Tutus & Cowboy Boots?

Find out more at:

http://authorcaseypeeler.com

About the Author

Casey Peeler grew up in North Carolina and still lives there with her husband and daughter.

Growing up Casey wasn't an avid reader or writer, but after reading Their Eyes Were Watching God by Zora Neal Hurston during her senior year of high school, and multiple Nicholas Sparks' novels, she found a hidden love and appreciation for reading. That love ignited the passion for writing several years later, and her writing style combines real life scenarios with morals and values teenagers need in their daily lives.

When Casey isn't writing, you can find her near a body of water listening to country music with a cold beverage and a great book.

Connect with Casey

Website: http://authorcaseypeeler.com

Shop: https://squareup.com/market/author-casey-peeler

Instagram: www.instagram.com/caseypeeler

facebook: www.facebook.com/caseypeelerauthor

twitter: www.twitter.com/AuthorCasey

tumblr: http://caseypeelerauthor.tumblr.com

Pinterest: http://www.pinterest.com/authorcasey/

Goodreads: http://www.goodreads.com/author/show/7106874.Casey_Peeler

YouTube: https://www.youtube.com/channel/UColmpt4hErNau1woOOsJOnw

Also by Casey Peeler

Full Circle Series (Losing Charley, Finding Charley & Loving Charley)

Full Circle Series Box Set

Southern Perfection

Crashing Tides

Covering the Carolinas

Our Song

Tutu's & Cowboy Boots Part 2

Boondocks

Made in the USA
Middletown, DE
09 September 2021